DEDICATION

Dedicated to Thomas Anthony Casoria, Firefighter Engine 22, New York City, who gave his life at age 29 to save fellow firefighters and citizens on September 11, 2001, South World Trade Tower.

ACKNOWLEDGMENTS

Anne Ponzio
Frank Ponzio
Carolyn Seibert
Nancy Oberst Soesbee

Thank you.

MICHAEL A. PONZIO

The novels listed below makeup the *Lover of the Sea* series. The title characters are historical.

- *Pontius Aquila: Eagle of the Republic*
- *Pontius Pilatus: Dark Passage to Heaven*
- *St. Pontianus: Bishop of Rome*

Each of the novels can be read alone, or chronologically. Every novel is based on a factual character in history, and embraces martial arts, capable women, and romance.

Cover photo: Pontius Pilate introduces Jesus, in this statue at the base of the Holy Stairs in Rome. Sculpted by Ignazio Jacometti in 1854 (1819-1883).
Attribution — Photo Credit: 14 November 2014, 09:59:00, Self-photographed by User:Rabax63. Licensed under the Creative Commons Attribution-Share Alike 4.0 International license, wikipedia.org/wiki/Creative_Commons
Changes: Bottom third cropped.

The History

Yosef ben Matityahu (Josephus), Jewish historian, 70 A.D.:

At this time, there appeared Jesus, a wise man. For he was a doer of startling deeds, a teacher of the people who receive the truth with pleasure. And he gained a following both among many Jews and among many of Greek origin. And when Pilate, because of an accusation made by the leading men among us, condemned him to the cross, those who had loved him previously did not cease to do so. And up until this very day the tribe of Christians, named after him, has not died out.

The Annals by Roman Historian Publius Cornelius Tacitus:

[Emperor Nero accused to have caused the great fire in Rome in 64 A.D.] - To suppress this rumor, Nero fabricated scapegoats and inflicted the most extreme tortures on a class called Christians by the populace. Despite the Roman citizens' hatred for the Christians, they pitied the victims. Christus, from whom their name had its origin, suffered the extreme penalty during the reign of Tiberius at the hands of one of our procurators, Pontius Pilatus.

The Gospel of Mark– The Bible:

Very early in the morning, the chief priests, with the elders, the teachers of the law and the whole Sanhedrin, made their plans. So they bound Jesus, led him away and handed him over to Pilate. "Are you the king of the Jews?" asked Pilate.

"You have said so," Jesus replied.

The chief priests accused him of many things. So again, Pilate asked him, "Aren't you going to answer? See how many things they are accusing you of."

But Jesus still made no reply, and Pilate was amazed. "Do you want me to release to you the king of the Jews?" asked Pilate, knowing it was out of self-interest that the chief priests had handed Jesus over to him. But the chief priests stirred up the crowd to have Pilate release Barabbas instead.

"What shall I do, then, with the one you call the king of the Jews?" Pilate asked them.

"Crucify him!" they shouted.

"Why? What crime has he committed?" asked Pilate.

But they shouted all the louder, "Crucify him!"

Wanting to satisfy the crowd, Pilate released Barabbas to them. He had Jesus flogged, and handed him over to be crucified.

MICHAEL A. PONZIO

CONTENTS

1	FROM THE ASHES	1
2	THE BANQUET	20
3	A NEW HOME	35
4	LEAVING HOME	39
5	THE MEETING	50
6	BENEVENTUM	57
7	COMINIUM	63
8	THE LAST FIRE	71
9	RETURN TO ROME	79
10	SUA MANUS	88
11	GENTILES AND JEWS	101
12	CORINTH	115
13	SEA TO THE MOUNTAINS	135
14	AOSTA	154
15	THE PASS	170
16	A HOLE IN THE SKY	189
	AFTERWORD	197
	THE AUTHOR	200
	BIBLIOGRAPHY	201

MICHAEL A. PONZIO

1 FROM THE ASHES

Pontius Pilatus urged his horse to a gallop along the shadowy street. The night sky glowed red and fiery above the buildings. His devoted bodyguard Metellanus rode beside him. They burst from the dark street into a large plaza brilliant with flames. The square was bounded by insulae: the multiple-story tenement buildings which housed many of the citizens of Rome. Scores of men were fighting a fire that engulfed the wood frame buildings. On the far side of the square, citizens were rushing in all directions. As Pilatus and Metellanus dismounted, their senses came under assault. The flames had transformed the tenements into luminous orange and magenta edifices. The men's faces were hot from the radiant heat, while their backs remained cool from the March night. The odor of burning wood permeated the air and the plaza roared with the sounds of screaming people among a multitude of indistinguishable noises.

A convoy of two-wheeled carts careened into the plaza, pushed by Vigiles, the firemen and watchmen of Rome. As the carts rattled over the paving stones, leather buckets affixed with rope handles threatened to tumble out. Other carts raced by, containing pumps, called siphos, used by the fire brigades to douse the flames. Attached to the side of the carts were axes and long wooden staffs tipped with heavy iron hooks for tearing down the buildings in advance of a fire. Pilatus shouted to the leader of the

Vigiles, but the man failed to notice him. Pilatus grabbed the officer by the shoulder. "Centurion, where is Prefect Nigrinus?"

"I don't know. I just arrived here and we need to put water on this fire. I have a job to do!"

Amid the mayhem, the caravan of carts continued to speed by into the center of the plaza toward the fountain. The centurion started to follow them, but Metallanus blocked his path. Pilatus shouted above the din. "I also have a job to do and I must find him. Since Nigrinus is the prefect of the city's Vigiles and your commanding officer, I assume you can make a good estimate of his location."

The centurion pointed to the right side of the burning row of dwellings, where Vigiles had stretched out large sheets of sailcloth. They were catching the frantic inhabitants jumping from the upper stories. "The prefect always places life first. He will be there. I am leaving now to lead my men. If you have a problem with that, my name is Casorius Antonius."

He turned and ran to catch up with the last carts as they sped by. Pilatus, from habits formed in his military life, shouted encouragement, "Virtus, Centurion!"

As Pilatus and Metellanus threaded through the crowds in the plaza, Pilatus could hear Centurion Antonius bellowing commands to his men. "Watermen! Organize the citizens and form bucket brigades at the fountain! Pumpmen! Position your pumps over here! Take two squads of hookmen to those insulae before the fire spreads."

The Vigiles attacked an evacuated insula which was still void of flames and downwind of the fire. The hookmen punctured the outer plaster, pulled down the wooden beams of the first story, and retreated as the bottom of the five-story building caved in. They returned and repeated the process to further diminish the structure. Pilatus and Metellanus arrived upwind of the hookmen where the lower stories of several buildings were on fire. In the upper floors, people hung out of the windows to escape the smoke pouring out of the buildings. The high-pitched screams of women and children penetrated the din. Many were jumping onto sailcloths held taut by the Vigiles. Pilatus's cousin, Gaius Petronius Pontius Nigrinus, directed the rescue efforts. Pilatus clasped Nigrinus's shoulder and said, "Cousin, the catapults are still on the way. Where do you want them positioned when they arrive?"

Nigrinus pointed as he continued to assess the Vigiles' rescue endeavors. "See Antonius's hookmen? If they can't tear down more insulae before the fire spreads out of the plaza, the Vigiles will have dangerous work in those narrow streets. You insisted your idea would be faster and safer than using hookmen. Where are your damn catapults? You and your connections! Maybe you shouldn't have asked Macro to supply his artillery. And how are you going to be accurate enough? I need the lower floor destroyed first, not trial and error lofting rocks into the fire."

Pilatus, remembering his cousin had only served briefly as a tribune in the legions, answered, "The catapults we will use are the ballistae, the large crossbows that can throw iron spears and stones. They are very accurate."

Within seconds, above all the screaming and noise, Pilatus heard a loud command reminiscent of his days fighting on the empire's northern frontier in Germania: "Ballistae, throw!"

The reverberations sounded like swarms of bees whizzing toward the fire. He turned his head and followed the buzzing sounds toward the buildings on fire. A staccato of loud cracking sounds erupted from the snapping and splintering of wood. The bottom stories of several wooden insulae gave way as more of the flying projectiles impacted the shabbily built tenements.

Pilatus shouted, "Macro kept his word and sent the artillery!"

Carroballistae, the wheeled artillery of the legions, were lined up on the far side of the square. Piled next to the ballistae were stacks of stone shot, chiseled into orbs for accuracy and to use as ammunition against the insulae. Then panic suddenly engulfed Pilatus as he remembered Antonius and his men. He ran to warn them, hoping they were not near the bombardment, but stopped when he saw that the centurion had already pulled his men back. Additional volleys from the ballistae caved in more of the burning buildings. In addition to the carroballistae, smaller ballistae, the scorpions, complemented the barrage. The collapsed mass of an entire side of the plaza was burning and had to be extinguished with water. The watermen drew water faster than the rate supplied by the aqueduct feeding the plaza's fountain, but the fire was extinguished before the fountain ran dry.

Pilatus joined Nigrinus as he discussed plans for rescue and recovery. Near the mass of smoldering wreckage, he addressed a circle of his centurions, officers who commanded 80 Vigiles. Each of the seven districts of the city had a fire brigade, a cohort consisting of 480 Vigiles who served Rome, a city of over one million. When not fighting fires, the Vigiles were watchman and police.

Vestal Virgins, leading scores of female slaves, arrived to help the Vigiles and doctors administer first aid. As Nigrinus met with his officers, firemen spread out among the wreckage to rescue injured victims. With the next phase underway, Nigrinus then turned to Pilatus and said, "Thank you, cousin. Yes, I doubted you, but the ballistae arrived just in time. So, you convinced Macro to send them? And now I see using siege weapons is an excellent way to demolish buildings. Those flimsy tenements didn't have a chance. However, we could never use the carroballistae in narrow streets. What do we do then?"

Pilatus was quick to answer, "The smaller, portable ballistae should work. The scorpions can be carried on the back of a mule. I will talk to Macro and . . ." Pilatus heard a shout from Antonius, who was crouching amid the rubble, reaching into a pile of debris that had been the framework of a building. He helped an adolescent boy push his way free of the prison of wooden timbers, beams, and plaster. His face, arms, and legs were smudged with black streaks from the charred wood. The boy wore a tattered tunic, had no sandals, and his bulla, a tiny rawhide sack, hung on a leather cord around his neck. He shook his head bringing about a sudden alertness, a behavior that reminded Pilatus of a cat that had fallen, landed on its feet, and with quick looks in all directions, was deciding which way to run.

To be alive despite the crushing collapse of the building appeared impossible, but Pilatus knew the inhabitants of this poor Roman neighborhood were very resilient. He was sure the boy's survival had depended on a combination of skills gained by living on the streets, natural intuition, intelligence, and luck. The youth looked as if he were about to bolt, and Pilatus imagined the boy was like a stray cat, who suspected everyone as a threat. But the shock from his ordeal caused him to hesitate just long enough for Antonius to grab his hand. The boy's face flushed and a flood of tears burst forth.

#

At noon the next day, the last of the female patrons exited the morning session when the baths were reserved for women and girls. The Seni Public Baths were located at the edge of the Forum near the base of Palatine Hill, and included a gymnasium, library, food shops, massage facilities, and cold and warm baths.

Pilatus enjoyed the warmth of the sunny March afternoon as he waited with Metallanus in front of the baths for his cousin Nigrinus. Since returning to Rome from Judea several months earlier, he had been spending most of his mornings in the Forum, introducing himself to citizens and trying to develop new clients. He would then return home and have lunch with his wife Procula. In the afternoon, he continued his daily routine and went to the thermae, and sought out more clients. Pilatus recalled how this now normal routine contrasted to the first month after his return to Rome. *Tiberius ordered that I return to Rome because the Samaritans had accused me of committing a massacre. How ridiculous, when all I was doing was conducting a legal military action against an armed uprising! Tiberius died the day before my return. Then it was stressful waiting for Caligula's verdict. But fate was on my side! He excused me from the allegations.*

Nigrinus arrived and Pilatus noticed that his cousin's tunic was streaked with perspiration and grime. Pilatus laughed. "Cousin! What have you been doing? You need a bath!"

"That is because I was out doing real work, training with the Vigiles and honing their firefighting skills, while you have spent your morning socializing in the Forum." They embraced, and slapped each other on the back.

"Nigrinus, are you too exhausted? Do you want to clean off and go straight to the thermae and forego exercising?"

"And miss teaching you a lesson in wrestling? No! Let's go." Nigrinus slung his arm across his cousin's shoulders as they passed through the entrance bordered by Corinthian columns. In the changing room, he pulled his tunic over his head and handed it to an attendant. Nigrinus gave the bath employee, who was a Vigile, two copper coins, one for the entrance fee and one as a tip.

When not training or fighting fires, the Vigiles worked as attendants at the baths and guarded citizens' belongings while they were bathing. "Thank you, Prefect. I will wash and dry your tunic. When do you want it ready?"

The attendant handed them each a strigil to remove sweat before they entered the bath. Nigrinus said, "You are in Casorius Antonius's century, am I right?"

"Yes, I am a hookman in Vosillus's squad."

"Your men did an excellent job yesterday, coordinating with the Praetorians' ballistae."

"Thank you, sir. Stronzo, um, I mean, Vosillus, is an excellent leader. And using the ballistae is better than dodging falling timbers! Will artillery be used from now on? We could train to operate them and free the Praetorians."

"If I am in command, we will use the ballistae. That is a good suggestion to train the Vigiles. Oh, and I will be back in two hours for my tunic, thank you."

Pilatus and Nigrinus entered the gymnasium and Nigrinus chuckled as he said, "Vosillus's men call him Stronzo – 'Turdhead?' I want to see the look on his face when I call him that the next time I see him!"

Scores of Romans were wrestling in the gymnasium. The competition followed strict rules. Wrestlers could only use holds above the waist of the opponent and could not trip with their legs. The avocation was for health as much as the social interaction. Matches were held on padded mats.

Pilatus and Nigrinus had both warmed-up during wrestling matches with other middle-aged men. Then, Pilatus took on Nigrinus's challenge. "Cousin, let's see you back up your claim."

They both crouched and leaned forward, probing with their hands for a grasp. Nigrinus was a few inches taller and heavier. As Nigrinus stalked his smaller cousin, Pilatus avoided clinching as he shifted side to side. Nigrinus charged several times, but Pilatus moved sideways, and each time deflected his cousin's attack. Nigrinus rushed with more fervor. Pilatus turned his torso enough to avoid being seized and grasped Nigrinus's head with both hands. With his opponent's momentum and the leverage of his hip, he flipped the larger man over on his back. Before Pilatus could follow up, Nigrinus regained his feet and yelled, "You can't run forever!"

Nigrinus timed one of Pilatus's evasions and caught him in a face-to-face bear hug, locking both arms behind his cousin's back. As he tried to twist free, Pilatus rotated his torso, but Nigrinus tightened his grip and held on. He lifted his cousin off the floor and slammed Pilatus down. Pilatus turned his head as he fell, keeping his face from smashing into the mat, and broke the fall with his forearms. Nigrinus followed him to the floor and attempted to pin Pilatus on his back. His smaller cousin scrambled free and looped an arm behind Nigrinus's elbow, grabbed his shoulder with the other hand and bent his arm up and behind in a hammer lock. Using the leverage of his two-hand lock, Pilatus tried to induce enough pain to force Nigrinus to the floor. Instead, his sparring partner showed great strength and he rose to his feet. Nigrinus reached over and hooked his free arm around Pilatus's head. The pair stopped their struggle, both in precarious positions. Nigrinus forced out his words as he winced from the hammerlock. "It looks like my headlock wins!"

Pilatus strained a muffled reply from the pressure on his head. "Don't make me break your arm to show who won!"

"All right, all right. I agree. I would prefer not to try a throw or pin. We old men will call it a draw. Until tomorrow!"

Before plunging into the tempered water pool, they used strigils to remove the sweat from their bodies, scraping themselves with the utensils. Between scrapings, they rinsed off the curved utensils in a shallow channel with a continuous stream of warm water. The water discharged to the public toilets for reuse. After a quick dip in the pool, they joined a throng of men in the hot pool and relaxed listening to discussions on politics, women, and the world. Nigrinus looked at his cousin and smiled when they overheard a nearby man make a toast. Raising his cup of wine, he said. "Wine, women, warmth, to life destruction give, but it is by wine, women, warmth that we live!"

Pilatus closed his eyes and enjoyed the hot bath. "Mmm . . . I could stay here all day."

"Pilatus, you needed those wrestling matches, since you have an easy job, just talking all day with clients. Why don't you join me in training the Vigiles? We can make up for all the time we missed when you were in Judea."

Pilatus frowned. "Right now, I want a less stressful vocation. Governing the Hebrews was difficult. They complained about everything. I tried to please them. I built an aqueduct in Jerusalem, one of the measures to introduce them to our civilization, but they still refused to be Romanized."

Nigrinus nodded and tapped a knuckle on his forehead. "So, the Jews are hard-heads! Too bad your efforts didn't work. If we'd had them as allies in our legions, Rome would have conquered Persia by now!"

"Yes, they are a race of hard-heads, or as the Hebrews themselves would say: stiff necks."

"And what of the religious prophet named Jesus? You tried to follow the law and serve him Roman justice, but couldn't deal with the Hebrew religious leaders?"

Pilatus's mouth tightened and he cuffed his cousin on the back of the head. "Hey! You are the only person who could have said that without me becoming furious, dear cousin. I do not even talk to Procula about it. It is too sensitive a topic."

"Maybe you *should* talk about it, cousin!"

Pilatus appeared to calm down and Nigrinus said, "Does it surprise you that people today continue to follow Jesus's teachings?"

"Yes, I am surprised. Jesus barely talked to me. He wanted to be martyred. His followers fled during his trial and execution and then surfaced later, only to be persecuted by other Jews. They did not give me any trouble. It was as though he was using me and did not want to be freed. Yes, I finally gave up. I also feared reprisals from Tiberius after he accused my mentor Sejanus of conspiracy and executed him. And Nigrinus, I didn't thank you for your letters when I was in Judea. I would not have known the extent of Tiberius's paranoia that led to the execution of Sejanus's entire family."

Nigrinus answered, "Of course, cousin. We did what we could here in Rome to distract Tiberius from implicating you with Sejanus. When Tiberius considered the Samaritans' grievance and called you back to Rome, he no longer had a rational mind. Instead of governing, he displayed strange and paranoid behavior, living as a recluse in Capri. And about the martyr? – Cousin, I think your wife Procula is attending some of the Christos meetings that are held in private homes."

"I suspected that and knew she favored his philosophy, but if she is safe and doesn't embroil me, I will not interfere. After the Hebrews arrested Jesus, she had a dream and warned me not to get involved with him. But what choice did I have? I remind myself that some women are infatuated with actors, some women with gladiators, and some with religious zealots. No, Roman justice was not served on that occasion. However, I granted a proper burial when one of their priests, by the name of Joseph, asked for his body. Joseph, yes, Joseph of Arimathea, he was one of the few Jews who seemed rational."

"Keep a level head, Pilatus. This world is full of thousands of misjudgments where people do not get what they deserve. It wasn't as if you yourself accused or arrested him. They backed you into a corner.

"Now let's get back to us working together. The ballistae you persuaded Macro to supply produced amazing results in putting out the fire in the Subura district. Pilatus, we also have other problems. During the last several fires, gangs have attacked the Vigiles. They are hired by unscrupulous contractors, and they will not withdraw their thugs unless paid off by the tenement landlords. Even if they are not paid and the buildings burn, the contractors reap enormous profits to rebuild the tenement houses. You must have used urban riot methods to deal with the Hebrew conflicts. Vigiles can perform watch duties and policing against robbers, but they are not ready to fight these organized gangs. Will you consider training the Vigiles? My few years in the army as a staff tribune did not give me much experience."

As Pilatus stared ahead in thought, his lower lip curled. "I assume these hooligans you described ambushed the Vigiles. It was different in Judea. You would think they would have been satisfied because of Rome's tolerance of all religions. However, they were so sensitive to any infraction of their religion, that crowds still formed in dissent. The protests usually began peacefully, but had the potential to turn violent, so I ordered them to break up. They were fanatical. One time, I even threatened to have my legionaries slay them, but my bluff did not work and they refused to disperse. I did not want to kill them, but they needed to be punished. So on the next occasion, I blocked their exit from the plaza and had my men dressed in civilian clothing punish them with cudgels. In contrast, the Samaritans armed themselves, gathered outside the city, and refused to return to their homes. After a brief skirmish, I arrested their leaders, and per law, they were executed for sedition.

"But enough of reliving that time. So, Nigrinus, you have accepted your new role as Prefect of the Vigiles with great enthusiasm. Your command at the fire in the Subura plaza was efficient and effective. You have introduced a new way to use artillery by destroying the burning buildings. But aren't you angry that you were dismissed from the consulship? Prefect of the Vigiles is a demotion compared to being a consul."

"Yes, I was very proud to be the first of the Pontius gens to achieve consul. In the days of the Republic, that was the highest political office, but now consuls have no real political power. They preside over the Senate as facilitators, not political leaders. I was removed so Caligula could achieve more influence in the Senate. He then appointed his uncle Claudius and himself to the dual consul positions, replacing Proculus and me. Some people say Claudius is a halfwit and not a threat to Caligula's power. That is why he was appointed as co-consul. I am glad of the change. Now I am out in the city, actively doing things, not just sitting around listening to boring Senate debates that lead to no actions.

"Pilatus, we both know Macro well. You served with him in Germania. As Prefect of the Praetorian Guard he provided the ballistae to fight the Subura fire. Caligula, however, will not let the Praetorians leave him unprotected every time a fire occurs in Rome. The Seni bath attendant had a good idea, train the Vigiles to operate the ballistae. Even better, I should obtain funds to build our own artillery. And as for fighting the gangs, talk to Macro to develop ways the firefighters could defend themselves. He helped before. Go visit him."

#

Capella stirred from her nap. As she stretched the muscles along the entire length of her body, the involuntary action raised her consciousness just enough to perceive the most ecstatic feeling in the universe. Her eyes stayed closed through the moment and she was content, as she relaxed again and returned to her world of sleep. For Capella, her experiences as she slept were just as real as the waking world, and now the sleeping world was more intriguing.

She dozed, stretched out on the white marble balustrade and bathed by the warm Italian sun. The stone banister lined the entire training grounds of the Castra Praetoria, the permanent barracks of the Praetorian Guard, an elite force of Roman legionaries. Capella's favorite niche was on top of the balustrade. From there she could traverse and survey the entire grounds of the castra. Using the balustrade as her elevated walkway, she felt secure and safe from the feet of the hundreds of legionaries during their training activities.

Although immersed in the alternate world of her dreams, the subconscious recesses of her mind continued to monitor the surrounding environment. The cat's auditory senses identified and categorized many sounds. Her whiskers detected vibrations from the special force of Roman soldiers as they walked, marched, drilled, and sparred nearby. The Praetorian Guard's duty was to protect the Roman emperor, and her duty was to protect the castra's grain stores from rats and mice. Despite the noise and activity, she could still hear the slightest noise made by the rodents. She was aware in the way they scurried nearby that they were without fear now as she slept. In addition, Capella's olfactory nerves were sensitive enough to detect even the faintest and most diffuse odors. Her brain stored the identity of each scent, what creature had been nearby, and when the creature had been there.

In her dream world, she was an ancient member of her species in a land dominated by a huge river bordered with endless deserts. The great river's delta and marshes provided wonderful places to stalk and teemed with lively prey for her hunting pleasure. To Capella, this was paradise.

In Capella's perception, the Roman guards served her well. She was aware they had built the balustrade and the barrack's granary and assumed it was for her comfort and to attract mice for hunting. Although the soldiers occasionally provided food for her, it was never as tasty as a freshly killed warm and tender mouse, and she sometimes ate the handout to be deferential. Sometimes the guards would run their hands down her back. These wonderful massages were more invigorating than rubbing her back against a post. As she napped atop her balustrade, it was a convenient height for the legionaries as they walked by to apply a stroke across her back. Capella also assumed that the soldiers kept in check the large and dangerous animals that barked at her whenever they were nearby. She also thought they must be the soldiers' slaves since they were always eager to do whatever the soldiers commanded.

Life was good at the Castra Praetoria, but the people in her desert dreamland were more than good servants. The people of the desert land did not just serve but worshiped cats as gods and goddesses. As long as cats existed as a species, this memory would be passed across time from generation to generation and shape their descendants' behavior.

#

It had been several days since the Subura fire. Pilatus and Metellanus headed for an appointment with Prefect Macro at the Castra Praetoria, adjacent to the northeast gate of Rome. The training facilities housed the Praetorian Guard, whose primary duty was to provide security for the emperor, now Caligula.

They walked upon a road paved three hundred years earlier. The moisture from an early morning rain glistened on the flat stones of the street and was now drying up as the day became warm, sunny, and comfortable. There were no puddles of water pooled along the road. Roman engineers ensured their roads drained well, were straight, and endured.

Returning to the Castra Praetoria for the first time in ten years, Pilatus wondered, "*I was second in command to Sejanus the last time I was at the camp. Most of the time he was in Capri advising Tiberius. So, I was the de facto commander, until Tiberius reassigned me to Judea. I wonder how many of the men who used to serve are still at the camp?*"

Pilatus and his companion arrived at the front gate of the Castra Praetoria. Pilatus wore a tunic and a leather belt with a brass buckle which displayed an image of a boar, the Pontius clan crest. The metal armbands revealed his Samnite heritage. Although he was a knight, a member of the Roman equestrian rank, he wore a toga only for formal occasions. On his right hand he wore a gold ring, affixed with a red garnet and a green garnet. Two rings were on the ring finger of his left hand: his gold wedding band and an iron ring that signified Roman citizenship. As Pilatus and his escort entered the castra courtyard, the guards at the gate were playing bocce and merely glanced at them.

The Castra Praetoria, composed of buildings and training grounds, was in stark contrast with the wooden palisades and ditches that defined a Roman military camp in the field. Barracks, storerooms and offices formed three sides of the gravel training ground. Porticos supported by columns fronted the buildings. A paved walkway ran the length of the porticos, lined by a white marble balustrade. Roof tiles of terracotta covered the walkways and buildings.

In the courtyard, pairs of men sparred using wooden swords. Groups of men practiced fighting in formation using rectangular shields and wooden swords. Legionaries thrust and slashed at stationary targets with short swords. Some targets were mechanical devices which rotated upon impact. Other men, wearing armor, jumped onto or vaulted over wooden horses. While the legionaries in the Roman army derived their hardiness from time spent constructing roads and other civil projects, the Praetorians concentrated on practicing and developing their military skills to higher levels.

Pilatus, once a Praetorian Guard, now felt inadequate as he observed them practice. However, these thoughts faded as he recognized an old friend, Centurion Rittutus Phillipus, training Praetorians in hurling the javelin, called a pilum. Pilatus fondly remembered using the weapon hunting wild boars as he was growing up in Samnium. He waited for Phillipus to pause from their target practice and then approached the group of men. Phillipus, his back to Pilatus, faced a half circle of Praetorians as he demonstrated the proper grip for throwing the pilum.

Without turning, Phillipus flung the pilum over his back toward Pilatus. As the javelin spun through the air like a windmill blade, Phillipus turned and shouted at Pilatus. "Live up to your Samnite name, old man, and show these sorry grunts how to hit the boar's head!"

Pilatus intercepted the pilum with his right hand as it arced through the air and without breaking his stride, swung his right arm toward the target and trusted his senses. A split-second before he released the pilum, his eyes focused on a knot in a wooden beam beyond the target. An image of the pilum finding the target flashed in his mind's eye. He released the pilum. As it sliced into the target on a mound of soft sand, a pffffft sound occurred as the point threaded the jaw bone of the boar skull.

Phillipus guffawed and pounded Pilatus on the back. "You are still a lucky bastard! Men, see if you can match that! Some of you were just children the last time Pontius Pilatus, the former Prefect of Judea, was here as commander. Here is a history lesson for you. Like his kin in southern Italy, he grew up using the pilum, protecting his herds and hunting wild boar. Pilatus's grandfather was the first to earn the nickname Pilatus. He was so proficient with the pilum, he was selected to train the Roman legions in the use of the weapon, and his fellow legionaries gave him the name Pilatus. Now it is your turn. Soldiers! I want to see improvement in your accuracy."

The Praetorians returned to practice as Pilatus and Metellanus watched Phillipus work his men. Pilatus smiled as he reminisced about the veteran centurion.

"I remember when we served together in Germania. Phillipus was a good leader. He had the complete trust of his men. They would follow him anywhere. That man saved many lives on the battlefield. His quick wit and actions compensated for several of my own failed strategic decisions."

A Praetorian tribune, Cassius Chaerea joined them. Chaerea embraced Pilatus and introduced himself to Metellanus. "Pilatus! I thought you retired?"

"Chaerea, how are you? It's been a long time, comrade, since we served together in Germania."

"As good as can be, considering the changes in leadership. Couldn't stay away, huh? You got sick of all that political stuff in Judea?"

"Hmm, we'll see. Macro is expecting me."

Chaerea led Pilatus into the main building of the complex that served as the headquarters of the Praetorian Guard. They entered a large room lit by skylights, which was the office of the Prefect of the Praetorian Guards, Naevius Sutorius Macro. The prefect stood as he studied several scrolls rolled out on a table. Macro looked up and said, "Greetings, Pontius Pilatus. Forgive me for not meeting you in the courtyard. The emperor has me on a tight schedule to review and approve security for his new villa. And, I heard the use of the carroballistae was a success at the Subura fire."

Pilatus almost saluted by pounding his fist to heart and shouting virtus, but sensed the informality and refrained. "Thank you, a thousand times, Macro. The fire was contained and extinguished with your help. Nigrinus was pleased. We need your advice on another problem. Can you help train the Vigiles to protect themselves against bands of armed brutes? I'd like to apply your Praetorian urban tactics to train Nigrinus's men to rout the street thugs that have been attacking the Vigiles."

Macro replied, "Pilatus, you are being too humble. When we served together in the north, you were an excellent leader. And didn't you apply urban tactics in Judea? No matter, even if your cousin Nigrinus was not Prefect of the Vigiles, it would be my pleasure to grant full approval. Tribune Chaerea will assist you. After you draw up your plans, come by and review them with me."

The prefect returned to studying his diagrams. The succinct exchange with the prefect pleased Pilatus. As he turned to leave, he noticed the end of one of the large scrolls on the prefect's desk was held from rolling shut by a white furry object. It was a cat napping with forepaws and hind legs folded under its body. He would not have given it a second glance, except he remembered when he was prefect, there was a white cat named Bianca that lived in the barracks. The cat had irritated him by always insisting on curling up right on his scrolls under his nose when he was at his desk working. In time, Pilatus had welcomed the creature's company on those long and tiring nights at his desk.

Macro looked up and appeared irritated, but his expression calmed as he reflexively petted the sleeping cat.

"Do you recognize Bianca? She has been a fixture here for many years, but she is no longer interested in fulfilling her duties as a mouser. She has retired to be a scroll weight." He laughed. "Bianca handed her duties over to Capella, who lives on the balustrade surrounding the training grounds."

2 THE BANQUET

Pilatus arranged a meeting with Chaerea for the next day. He and Metellanus departed the castra and made their way through the crowded streets. Pilatus experienced the recurring fears that had plagued him months earlier. *I am certain Tiberius had planned a severe punishment for me, but the turn of events was amazing. Caligula sent the Samaritan delegation back to the east, promising them he would send me into exile. After they left, instead of a harsh judgment, he merely decreed that I could not hold office or lead a public life. What luck! What a relief! Besides, I am so tired of politics.*

Pilatus forced aside the dark thoughts and returned to the present as he said, "Metellanus, what a beautiful day to walk the streets of Rome!"

"Yes, Dominus."

"Why are you still being formal? Didn't I tell you to call me by my name? We are friends."

"And I greatly appreciate your friendship. But as a slave it is a habit, and I am afraid I will accidentally address you informally with your peers present."

"Don't worry about it, Metellanus. I was just thinking about formalities, but the formalities of political life. I am through with politics. I will retire and lead a casual life. Perhaps I will study philosophy and history."

"Yes, it is a good day, Dom . . . um, P-Pilatus! You enjoyed seeing old friends and your request to train the Vigiles was approved! But you studying philosophy? I will see it when I believe it!"

Pilatus laughed. "That's more like it Metellanus – that's more like a friend. Forget the formalities. And good joke!"

"Joke? Yes, but I meant I will believe it when I see it. Funny, but not intended."

"I don't know, Metellanus. I think sometimes words slip out that might have deeper meaning. Julius Caesar said, 'People only believe what they want to believe.'"

Metellanus paused to concentrate.

"Hmm. Yes, I see what you mean."

Pilatus said, "Look at the people's faces around us. Don't they look happy? The gloom of Tiberius's reign as emperor is over. In Caligula's first month of governing, he awarded reimbursements to citizens who had been unfairly harmed by Tiberius's tax system. Now months later, he has destroyed Tiberius's list of those wanted for treason and has recalled exiles back to Rome."

Metellanus added, "I heard he gave large cash bonuses to every member of the Praetorian Guard."

"Yes, buying loyalty is disgusting, but it may have avoided bloodshed, or worse, a civil war. But many people are pleased that Caligula has taken over after Tiberius's death. Romans think Caligula will be like his late beloved father, Caesar Germanicus, who became famous for his campaigns against the Germans."

"Pilatus, when Caligula assumed power, his name was written on the bulletins in the forum as Gaius Julius Caesar Germanicus. Why is he called Caligula?"

"Caligula grew up accompanying his father on military campaigns in Germania. As an infant, he wore a miniature legionary's uniform, including a small pair of caliga, the hobnailed military boots worn by the soldiers. He raised the soldier's morale and amused them as he marched about the camp attired in his uniform. They gave him the nickname Caligula, or "Little Boots." People do not use his nickname around him. He hates the name. After Caligula's father died, his grandfather Tiberius adopted him. Caligula has done well during his first few months. Let us hope he will be more like his father than like Tiberius."

As Pilatus and Metellanus arrived home, one of the male slaves, the doorkeeper of his house, met him at the vestibule. "Dominus, a messenger from the emperor arrived. You are invited to a banquet at his villa this afternoon. Lady Procula is in her room getting ready."

Pilatus placed a trusting hand on Metellanus's shoulder and whispered, "Find out if there is any news I need to know before we arrive at the banquet."

Pilatus entered their master suite. Valeria, Procula's attendant slave and close friend, helped her into her stola, a long dress. He never got tired of his wife's beautiful figure. She was nineteen years younger than him. At forty-nine, Pilatus had stayed in good physical condition and was pleased he remained attractive to his younger wife. Valeria left them alone as Procula looked over her jewelry. Pilatus kissed her on the back of her neck.

"You look beautiful as always." He was hoping they could spend time together before they left; however, she sensed his intentions.

"Please, later, love. The dinner is informal, so you can wear a long tunic instead of a toga. It is on the bed. I know you despise wearing a toga."

Pilatus washed his face and pulled the tunic over his head. It featured two vertical purple stripes on the left side of the tunic, indicating Pilatus's rank as an equestrian. He wrapped a cloth belt around his waist.

Procula tried on a necklace, as she said, "What happened today? Did Macro go along with your proposal?"

"Yes, I am happy to say he granted his approval."

"Wonderful, my love!"

"Yes, but I always wanted to distance myself from the political game of favors. I hope this support from Macro does not lead to something sour. The behavior of the Julii gens in their need for power is repulsive. It is public knowledge that Tiberius had members of his own family executed and had Caligula's parents and his male siblings put to death."

Procula added, "Don't you think Caligula must have lived for years in Tiberius's household, fearing he would have the same fate? What a contrast! I hope with the power he now holds, he will not let it go to his head."

Pilatus sat on the bed tying his sandals. "Everyone knows that

Macro and the Praetorian Guard support him because of the large sums of money he gave them. Those exiled Senators who have returned are now his political allies. We have all benefited from his reduction of the severe taxes imposed by Tiberius. However, he will never be as wise as his great uncle, Caesar Augustus. He promoted morality and advocated a return to strong family bonds."

Procula kissed her husband. "I agree, but let's discuss this later. We can at least enjoy the dinner. Your cousin Nigrinus will be there."

Well-off Romans typically traversed the city in litters carried by slaves. Wheeled traffic was usually not allowed during the daylight hours, due to congestion in the city. Caligula, however, had issued permission to use the popular two-wheeled coaches, no wider than a litter, for his attendees at the banquet. Procula and Pilatus sat in the small space behind Metellanus as he coaxed the roan mare down the street. Pilatus talked over the clopping hooves. "Metellanus, do you have any news for me?"

"My contacts at the villa told me that Caligula declared he is tired of listening to old men in the Senate. He announced he knows how to better spend Rome's treasury and talks of plans to build new villas. He is irritable and shouts at his servants for no particular reason."

Procula said, "But why the sudden change? Up to now he has been making prudent choices."

Pilatus stared ahead in thought, curling his lower lip. "During his first months of rule, the state business was backlogged due to Tiberius's lack of attention. The Senate pressed Caligula constantly for decisions, so he was preoccupied. Thus, he listened to his advisors in the Senate and made wise decisions. All the attention has made him pompous. Now after several months, the brashness of youth has surfaced. I had heard that Tiberius would not allow Caligula to leave at all during his residence at the imperial household in Capri. Caligula must have known and perhaps even participated in the obscene sexual parties that his uncle hosted. Thus, he lacks any moral upbringing, and now he realizes he has unlimited power. Instead of acting as a mature adult, he is driven by the uncontrolled lust of adolescence."

Metellanus continued, "Exactly. I was told he talks about making his lustful fantasies come true. He has invited some citizens with no political power or influence to the banquet with the intent to appear as a friend, but he actually covets their wives."

#

Pilatus and Procula arrived at Caligula's villa and were escorted through the atrium to the courtyard, a domed peristylium. A transom topped the dome, which provided natural lighting. Located beneath the skylight at floor level was a pool which collected rainwater. Like most Roman houses, the pool was connected to an underground cistern. Pipes from an aqueduct also provided running water to the villa, common for the homes of wealthy Romans. A fountain was located at the pool, creating the pleasing sound of splashing water. The marble floor, inlaid with a mosaic of a large peacock, was bordered by columns running the entire circumference of the circular room. Other rooms fronted the round courtyard.

The guests reclined on couches around the fountain while eating and drinking. Pilatus noted that Caligula lounged next to his youngest sister, Drusilla. *It is probably true that she has openly taken the role as his wife, after years of rumors of their secret, incestuous relationship. Was I influenced by Metellanus's comments or am I imagining that Caligula is wantonly gazing upon the young wife of Tribune Cassius Chaerea?* Caligula then stared at Prefect Macro's wife, Silvia, who reclined across the room, enjoying the delicacies. *He looks as if he is about to leap across the room at her right now. Perhaps he will look at Procula with lust, but that is as far as it will ever get.*

After the main courses were completed, Drusilla announced she would recite some poetry. As she recited poems by Horace, Quintus Horatius Flaccus, Procula whispered to Pilatus. "I am surprised. She was rather eloquent. However, my enjoyment is soured by the fact she lives as her brother's wife."

After dinner, the men gathered near the fountain to drink wine. Drusilla led the women into the adjacent study to sip on sweet almond liqueur.

Caligula raised his cup to Nigrinus. "To Prefect Nigrinus! An excellent strategy at the Subura fire. Success! The ballistae saved the day!"

Nigrinus held up his wine. "And let's drink to Macro for providing the equipment and men! Employing these new tactics is just the start. It has been ten days since the Subura fire. We should use these periods when we are not fighting fires to develop more firefighting innovations. The carroballistae launched heavier loads, but it will be difficult to use them for fires in narrow streets. We must depend more on the scorpions since they are small enough to move through the narrowest streets. Emperor, at your convenience, I would like to discuss fabricating our own ballistae and training the Vigiles to operate them."

Caligula's tone changed to concern, "Hmm. Maybe, Nigrinus, but how about the water? I heard that there was trouble with the water supply."

"Yes, Caesar, it appears we are finding this problem at other locations in the city. We had pumped and bucketed more rapidly than the fountain could supply and almost ran out of water. After the fire, we checked upstream of the fountain and we found several houses with pipes tapped into the aqueduct."

"Did these connections have permits?"

Nigrinus hesitated, but then answered, "No, as expected, the houses were owned by plebeians. We are checking other districts for illegal taps."

#

In the women's group, one of the patrician wives discussed their recent calling at various temples in Rome. "Oh Drusilla, Lucia and I felt a strong spiritual presence today at the temple of Venus. The new statues were so beautiful and the scents from the sweet incenses were delectable. We wore our most beautiful stolas to honor Venus. The goddess must have been impressed since the priest predicted continued prosperity and success for our husbands."

Lucia added, "And you should go up the Capitoline to see how they rebuilt Juno's temple . . ."

Drusilla interrupted. "You really think the priests can read the future? I'll bet the prophecies are as bounteous as the huge fees you pay those priests."

Lucia straightened her back and tilted her chin upward. "Drusilla, the gods have favored Rome for hundreds of years because our ancestors have honored the gods and goddesses of the Roman State. To stay in the gods' favor we and our descendants must continue to honor them to keep Rome strong. And the Roman home and family itself depends on the Vestals keeping alight the sacred flame of the goddess Vesta. As the Princep's consort you must be a devoted follower."

Drusilla answered, "I have always thought the patricians honored the gods and attended the temple ceremonies to impress the plebs and slaves. Of course, we all know the lower classes, being uneducated, pray to the gods out of fear and despair. Were not Augustus and Tiberius respected as gods? They were living gods, with such powers that they had real command over the workings of the world and millions of people's lives. Why do I need to go to the temple, when my own deified brother is right here?"

Macro's wife, Silvia, looked around at the women as she said to Drusilla, "There has always been room in the Roman pantheon for many Roman gods and goddesses. Also, people of other cities in the empire worship their own patron god or goddess. I do not see any problem with honoring the ancient gods as well as giving respect to your brother."

The women sipped their sweet drinks in silence. Procula felt uncomfortable as she thought, *Yes, Rome has had a reputation for allowing religious freedom of those it conquered. It was good for business. Augustus and Tiberius had been rather liberal in not requiring conquered subjects to worship them. I remember the extreme pressure Tiberius put on Pilatus to not offend the Jews when we were in Judea. And the creation of temples and the deification of Augustus and Tiberius has been the work of groups wanting to gain influence, not the emperors' ideas.*

Lucia broke the silence. "Rome is importing other deities from Egypt and from the Eastern religions. You would think we had enough gods and goddesses. With each new wave of legionaries returning from the wars in the East comes another new and exotic religion. After Julius Caesar returned from Egypt, people in Rome started worshiping a cat goddess named Isis. They treat living cats as gods and build monuments to them. Can you imagine that, worshiping cats?"

At this, most of the women laughed. Silvia added, "Yes, the Egyptians are fanatic about cats. Did you hear about the man in Egypt who ran over a cat while he was driving a chariot through the Alexandrian market? It was an accident, but an angry mob pulled the unfortunate driver from the chariot and beat him to death before anyone knew what happened. Romans may not worship cats, but we place great value in them. We are so used to them and forget how important their role is in protecting the granaries. The legions always make sure they take a pair of cats along to their frontier camps to keep the rats and mice from devouring their food stores."

Lucia responded, "With Silvia, it's cats, cats, cats. Silvia always talks about cats. The last time I visited her house, they were sitting, sleeping, and preening everywhere. Why, it's as if she decorates with cats!"

Drusilla laughed along with the ladies. "I am sure Silvia doesn't have any mice."

An attendant poured more liqueur for the women as Drusilla said, "Procula, you have been in Egypt, can you tell us about Isis?"

"Pilatus and I stopped in Alexandria for several weeks on our way to Judea. That was over ten years ago. I do remember that Isis is not a cat goddess nor represented as a cat. Isis is the Egyptians' goddess of creation. They consider the cat an embodiment of Bastet, the Goddess of Fertility. I was told their cats are embalmed and mummified, the same as the Egyptian royal families." Several women giggled.

Drusilla said, "Procula, your knowledge on religions is commendable. Did you know my brother just approved the building of a temple to Isis in Rome? However, he only approved a site removed from the holy area of the Forum where the State temples are located. You must have also learned something about the Jewish religion while you were in Judea. Did you meet the rebel Jesus? I understand some of the Jews think he was god born in man."

Procula's face turned crimson as she thought about her weekly visits to her friends' houses where they discussed the teachings of Jesus. She wondered if any of the women suspected her habits. Not wanting to threaten her husband's standing, she was too nervous to tell a convincing lie. She calmed herself and decided to tell at least some truths.

"I did see him preach in Judea. He advocated that we love everyone, friends, strangers, and even enemies. He said that was the way to peace. Spirit was more important than wealth."

At this there were snickers and chuckles from the group of women, but she continued, "His preaching severely upset the leaders of the Jews."

Drusilla said, "What did your husband think about him? Imagine what would have happened if Pilatus had not crucified him. If we followed Jesus's advice, we would just give away everything we had and then we would all become paupers and slaves!"

At this, most of the women laughed. Procula's self-control faltered and she might have recovered if she had remained quiet for a few seconds. But instead she burst into tears. She looked at the floor and said, "They never proved to Pilatus he was a threat to Rome. The Jewish priests wanted him executed because he threatened their own power. My husband is sensitive about Jesus and I would be too afraid to remind him about that ordeal."

Drusilla, fearing her guests would remember her first dinner party with disdain rather than as being entertaining, tried to dismiss the subject as trivial. "Procula, I am sorry, that's just boring man-business. Pilatus was simply keeping the Jews happy so they wouldn't make trouble. All our husbands have to do things like that."

She waved at one of the slaves and soothing music from several flutes and lyres echoed across the domed room. Just as the relaxing music seemed to take effect, a centurion of the Vigiles appeared at the entrance to the peristylium. He talked excitedly with several guards. The centurion surveyed the banquet guests and nodded at Nigrinus who joined the animated discussion. The guests' conversations quieted, and the music stopped.

Nigrinus and the centurion walked across the mosaic of the peacock and approached the circle of guests. In the silence, a tapping staccato from the hobnails on the bottom of the centurion's caliga reverberated across the room. Nigrinus nodded at the Vigile. The centurion saluted and addressed the group of men.

"Virtus! Emperor, consuls, honorable prefects, a fire has started in the Aventine. We put it out after several blocks burned, but other fires have been started, we believe intentionally. When several cohorts responded to the new fires, gangs attacked the Vigiles. It's a running fight. We still do not have control of the fires."

Nigrinus addressed Caligula as the group of men listened intently. They included Prefect of the Praetorian Guards, Naevius Sutorius Macro; Prefect of Granaries, Gancius Petronius; and Tribune Cassius Chaerea.

"Emperor, I will need to bring in Vigiles cohorts from the other districts. I request that Macro send Praetorians to protect the Vigiles and bring the ballistae. May I have your approval?"

Caligula nodded.

Nigrinus continued, "And forgive me for leaving the banquet. I believe Pilatus and I can manage the problem. Excuse us while we ensure our wives have the proper bodyguards and entourage to safely return home."

Nigrinus looked to Pilatus and as they began to leave, Caligula said, "Pilatus, stay here. I will have a word with you."

Pilatus waved for Nigrinus to go on. Most of the men moved into the atrium to discuss how they were going to mobilize for the crisis. Caligula appeared aggravated as he walked toward Pilatus. Pilatus stood his ground as Caligula pushed an angry face uncomfortably close to his.

"Pilatus, I heard you wanted to help Nigrinus control the rioters that are interfering with the firefighters. Macro's Praetorians can take care of them. When I told you that you could not have a public life, I did not only mean elected or appointed positions. I intended for you to stay quiet and out of the public eye. When I heard about your display of bravado at the Castra today, I checked into your other doings. You are campaigning for clients! I consider that a public activity, which I forbade."

Pilatus's head spun. At first, he was dumbfounded that Caligula even cared about his plans. Then in an instant he felt the heat of fear spread across his whole body. It was just months ago when he came close to being executed by Tiberius, followed by the uncertainty of Caligula's judgment for the complaints made by the Samaritans. However, Pilatus now bristled with anger. He found it difficult to be scolded by this young, egocentric man.

Caligula waited for a response, but Pilatus remained silent. "You are exiled from Rome for one year. Leave the mainstream of Roman society. Don't you have members of your gens still in Samnium? Yes, that would be good. Go to Beneventum."

Caligula laughed as he added, "Better still, go, go . . . someplace back in the hills, and, ha, ha, ha . . . and shepherd the goats, like, like . . . your ancestors did. You have one week to leave."

Caligula was finished and started to walk away. Pilatus was so shocked by the suddenness of Caligula's demands that he stood there without responding. But his silence intensified Caligula's anger. He stopped, turned slightly toward Pilatus and snapped, "You dare not acknowledge my command? To make you remember who I am, you will leave tomorrow, alone, without your wife. And you can thank me for not imposing more severe punishment."

Pilatus submerged his anger and knew that now even the slightest sign of disrespect would be disastrous. He hid the fact he was grinding his teeth as he controlled his voice, and answered firmly, "Absolutely, as you command, Caesar."

Late afternoon shadows cast by the emperor's villa darkened the street as Pilatus escorted Procula to their waiting coach. In this wealthy part of patrician Rome, the teeming crowds of the plebeian neighborhoods were absent. The walls of the houses were clean and bare of the extensive graffiti that was present throughout most of Rome. Pilatus wondered if Procula could tell he was uneasy. Metellanus waited in the driver's seat as they squeezed into their carriage. Pilatus thought, *Procula's silence signifies she senses my distress. She usually lets me talk first when I am troubled.* They sat silently in the small compartment as the horse's hooves tapped on the pavement. As his adrenaline subsided, Pilatus said, "My love, the emperor is sending me out of town on state business. I must leave tomorrow. I thought we could spend the evening together before I leave."

Procula sighed, "This was not what I expected. The way you

acted, I thought something terrible had happened. I am relieved you didn't have to go to the fire and that the banquet ended early. Now we can have time alone."

They both remained silent for the rest of the way home, as Pilatus's thoughts turned to love-making, which he suspected was on her mind as well. He drove the conversation he had had with Caligula out of his mind. *No reason to spoil our time together. I'll tell her afterwards.*

3 A NEW HOME

She huddled in the corner of the kitchen. *I hurt so much and my head is throbbing! And they have not guessed I am really a girl. When I was rescued, I could not even remember my name. My own name. I forgot it again! No, no, it is Arena. My name is Arena! Now I remember . . . the fire, the building that collapsed, and the man who rescued me. He is Antonius, that's it, his name . . . Antonius.*

Antonius had returned from a day's work and his wife Livia was speaking her mind. "Casorius Antonius, you got home from training all day and they are calling you back again? You are exhausted! Every time you leave I am afraid I will never see my husband again! And what am I to do with this young street urchin you brought home, anyway? He sits on the floor and stares off at nothing. I ask him questions, but he will not talk. He has latched onto you like a chick just hatched from an egg."

"Livia, you know I have to go. These fires could even spread to our district if we do not get them under control now. I will be safe. Nigrinus has called out the Vigiles cohorts from the other districts. So, we will have plenty of men. But look Livia, the gods have sent us a fine son. Once we get to know each other better, he'll recover from his shock."

He kissed his wife and crouched next to the boy. "Young man, these last days have been hectic with one crisis after another. I didn't even take time to ask your name. I am Casorius Antonius. This is my wife, Livia. What is your name?"

Arena had disguised herself as a boy for years, after seeing what had happened to other orphan girls on the street. She answered, "I am Ar . . ." *They still think I am a boy!* "I am Arena, no . . ., uh, Arenus. I am Arenus."

Antonius looked up at Livia and smiled, then tousled the adolescent's close-cropped hair. "I will be back later. Mind Livia while I am gone."

Antonius left his house and moved quickly toward the Aventine quarter. Undetected by Livia, Arena slipped out of the house. She secretly followed Antonius as he jogged several blocks from his home and arrived at the municipal building where his Vigiles century mustered. Finding no one there, he saw a posting. He muttered aloud as he read, "Vigiles are to report to the Palatine Hill." He then realized the young orphan he had rescued was standing beside him. He did not look surprised and said, "Go back to the house."

Arena felt an unfamiliar urge to stay with Antonius. "I can show you a short cut to your men, come on!"

Arena ran down the street and glanced over her shoulder to see if he was following. Antonius joined her and they jogged at a steady pace along empty streets and alleys. After several minutes threading through the city, the light and roar of the Palatine fire became noticeable. Antonius looked around and could not find the youth.

Arena watched from the shadows as Antonius entered the Forum. The fire was along a street up the Palatine Hill, but the closest water source was the fountain at the Forum's plaza. Several Vigiles were dipping leather buckets into the pool surrounding the fountain and passing them hand to hand across the plaza. The bucket line was comprised of citizens and included a few Vigiles. Most of the firemen were dousing the fire or pulling down the burning buildings to form firebreaks. As Antonius joined in to help the bucket line, he shouted encouragement to keep the water moving. Arena heard a commotion behind her and looked to see a group of men, some carrying sticks, rushing toward the plaza. By their looks, she knew they were not coming to help. Just as she shouted a warning to Antonius, the men crashed into the citizen bucket brigade. Many the people fell from the blindsided onslaught of the attackers. Others sustained injuries as they were clubbed.

Antonius was furious. With no measure of caution, he waded into the mass of assailants, swinging two buckets of water in wide circles, the rotating weight spinning him. Antonius cleared out an area around him as the impact of the buckets, each heavy with water, knocked out several of the attackers. The commotion attracted the rest of the hoodlums and they surrounded him beyond arm's length. Most of the water had spilled out of the pails and he continued to flail at the air with the limp buckets. Amid the melee of the noise and fire the thugs broke into laughter. Antonius paused, and then assaulted the largest brute with the fury of a human tornado. The bold, unexpected attack caught them off guard and they froze. Antonius trapped the adversary's club, entangling it in the rope handle of one bucket. He swung the other bucket around the thug's neck, smashed his knee into the man's chest and slipped behind him trapping the man's arms, then using him as a shield. It was so sudden, the other thugs who tried to hit Antonius with cudgels, bludgeoned Antonius's captive instead.

Antonius dropped the deadweight as several other thugs cracked their cudgels over his back. He spun around, swinging both buckets upward, which cleared their weapons. The buckets obstructed their vision and his low kicks crumpled them to the ground. Antonius screamed to the citizens,

"FIGHT! FIGHT THEM!"

The onlookers recovered from the initial attack, overcame their fear, and retaliated. They had tough adversaries, however and the thugs waded into the crowd swinging their weapons.

Arena saw the Praetorians arrive across the plaza. She ran to the soldiers, pointing as she shouted, "There is a gang of outlaws at the fountain killing people!"

The tribune in charge turned to his centurion, "Phillipus, form two squads here and wait for my signal."

Arena was anxious, wondering why they were waiting. She tried to run to the fountain, but the centurion grabbed her and told a citizen to detain her. The Praetorians made ready and she heard a high-pitched whistle from the far side of the plaza. The Praetorians charged toward the fountain, and the crowds gave way. Antonius stumbled away from the fight and helped several of the injured citizens out of the fracas. As he turned to look back toward the fountain, Arena hugged him from behind. Antonius said, "They were slaughtering us! We are fortunate the Praetorians came. None of those thugs will escape."

The Praetorian guards had not engaged until they had their quarry surrounded. They showed no mercy. Those few louts who escaped were the only survivors.

4 LEAVING HOME

Pilatus cherished the quiet of the garden in the early morning. He sat on the stone bench, palms resting on his knees. Lush growth encompassed the fountain pool which attracted song birds in constant motion from bush to bush. His gaze fixed on the surface of the pool. *I can never let Caligula know how much he is punishing me with this exile from Procula.* Before he had married Procula he had known other women, but every time he was with her, it reminded him that all those affairs in his earlier years had been merely attractions.

Wherever men assembled at the public baths and other social gatherings, the boasting of their intimate contacts with women was a popular pastime. Pilatus's casual acquaintances wondered why he did not join in and talk of his personal sex life, and they pestered him about it. Although Pilatus did not have affairs with other women, it was none of anyone else's business.

Pilatus was drawn to his wife as his thoughts surfaced. He entered their bedroom. Procula awoke, as sparrows sang near the fountain just outside their bedroom. She opened her eyes and said with a sleepy smile, "It was so perfect last night!"

"It was. Like always!"

Procula sat up, now wide awake. "We were married eleven years ago, today! I almost forgot. I was nineteen and you were thirty-eight. I remember that I was anxious. You were an older man and then right away you took me to Judea away from my family. But our first night together was wonderful and has been ever since.

"Mother had also coached me about the likely ways the marriage would change after the first few months. Husbands will be with other women, and I assumed you had taken this path. I knew you cared for me, but thought you had just been very discreet. At first I tried to detect if you had been with any other women, but I found a way not to care. When they assigned you to Judea and you wanted me to go, I knew you loved me. I stopped caring about whether there were other women."

"There are no others, Procula." Pilatus sat down on the bed close to his wife and placed one arm around her waist. "Last night I told you I was leaving on a state trip. When Caligula learned I was raising clients and helping Nigrinus, he became infuriated. As punishment, he has exiled me for a year. He has prohibited you from accompanying me."

Procula fell back on the bed and her eyes filled with tears. Pilatus comforted her and they lay together in a soundless, timeless, embrace.

After a quiet breakfast, their parting was quick. Both Procula and Pilatus disliked long goodbyes. Pilatus noticed she embraced him a final time for a moment longer than usual.

As Pilatus walked toward the front door he passed Rusticus, the mastiff guard dog that appeared to be asleep in his niche. Although Rusticus was well-mannered, it was the nature of his breed to exhibit fierce loyalty to his human family. He was a descendent of the interbreeding of two types of mastiffs. A hundred years earlier, Julius Caesar's invasion force had brought a larger Celtic strain from Britain to Italy. The Celtic mastiff was bred with the Neapolitan strain, known for its superior intelligence and loyalty. Breeding the two strains had produced a robust species which retained the intelligence and loyalty of the Neapolitan variety. The Romans used the mastiffs as guard dogs, but Rusticus's less fortunate cousins were forced to fight to their death at professional dogfights.

Rusticus appeared as if he would never notice an intruder. He looked a little ridiculous now. His eyes, bright with recognition, followed Pilatus's progress down the hallway. Otherwise, the dog remained motionless as his chin rested on his forepaws. Pilatus snickered, noting that the dog refused to move and disturb his companion Arcturus, the grey and white striped cat, who was napping on his back. As he exited the house he called back to the pair, "I know you ferocious animals will protect the house!"

Pilatus walked his horse along the paved street, and thought of his hurried exit from the city. He could have taken a comfortable coach, but he chose not to practice what he considered the soft habits of the wealthy. Pilatus's most loyal and dependable man, Metellanus, would stay in Rome to protect Procula, and Nigrinus would also be nearby. Pilatus insisted that Metellanus and several loyal slaves accompany Procula to her friends' houses where she attended the Christianos religious meetings. *She has become disappointed with the old and implausible pantheon of Greek and Roman gods. Those old gods' only value had been to unify the State. But why would these "gods" display the worst of the human traits as described in all their myths and legends? Would not a god be above these petty behaviors?*

I am supposed to meet two escorts and Nigrinus's son, Epiphanius, near the Porta Capena. It was Nigrinus's idea to take along Epiphanius for new experiences.

Pilatus continued through the crowded streets of the city, the saddle bags holding only his scrolls, a blanket, a few clothes and minimal food and water. He preferred to travel light and there would be inns along the way. As he passed through Porta Capena, the southeast city gate, he was still not at the limits of the city. Rome, like many of the empire's prosperous cities, had grown beyond the ancient walls. The populace no longer needed to fear foreign invaders, who were held at bay by Roman legions beyond distant frontiers.

The traffic on the road had diminished allowing Pilatus to now ride his horse. He passed a milestone showing he was heading south on the Appian Way. For economic and military reasons early in the republic, the Romans had built the road to link the city to their colonies and allies. *How ironic! This road contributed to the eventual defeat of my ancestors, the Samnites, after three wars with Rome.*

A shout brought Pilatus out of his musings. "Uncle! Stop, wait up!"

Pilatus reined his horse and saw Nigrinus's son, Epiphanius, accompanied by two of Nigrinus's slaves. The trio was a contrast of body types. Epiphanius was a teenager of medium build, light skinned with short brown hair and blue eyes. One of his companions was burly with dark eyes, dark complexion, and long hair. The other man was small and wiry with short curly hair. Pilatus nodded at the smaller man, who nimbly vaulted onto his horse and moved ahead of them down the road. The other man waited for Epiphanius to mount and move ahead, and then he followed.

Epiphanius was a well-educated young man, but he wanted to supplement his education with the experiences he imagined would come with travel. Pilatus remembered Epiphanius's tendency to talk for hours on end. He was the son of his first cousin, but it was common to call senior male cousins "uncle." Epiphanius said, "Uncle, thank you for taking me with you. I have studied Greek philosophy, rhetoric, and Greek and Roman literature, but I want to travel. Father said that you will study history on this sabbatical."

Pilatus answered, "Yes, I have an interest in the Jewish culture and want to learn more about their history."

"Father is proud of your service. He said you governed for over ten years in Judea and that prefects before you only lasted two or three years. My father is happy you returned to Rome, but he thought the reason the emperor called you back was wrong. I barely remember anything about you. Before you left, I was six or seven. Uncle, did you learn much about Judea?"

"It was difficult governing there, but I learned much about their culture. The Hebrews have written down their ancient history, which is interwoven with their religion. I was not able to procure any of their scrolls, because it was against Jewish law for me to possess any of their religious literature. However, Procula's uncle was governor of Egypt, and he obtained copies of a Greek translation of the Jewish Torah. The book is called the Septuaginta, and was translated by Greek-speaking Jews in Egypt."

"Did you bring these documents? May I read them? I can read and speak Greek."

Pilatus chuckled. "Of course, nephew. You will also be interested in stories about Mesopotamia that were originally written on clay tablets. Since Alexander's time, Greeks have lived in the region. There they found the ancient tablets and translated them into Greek."

"I am very excited about all of this, but what about family history? I feel fortunate that we will visit Samnium to learn about our family's origins. You were born there, am I right, Uncle?"

"Yes, and my late parents never left. However, your father's parents left Samnium and he was born in Rome."

Epiphanius said, "My grandfather told me that the Samnites and Romans were at war a hundred years ago. He said the Samnites were formidable adversaries and the Roman legions adopted their use of the pilum from them."

"Yes, Epiphanius, you are correct. There were three wars between the Romans and Samnites, forgotten about except by historians. But we are all Romans now. I mean we are all Roman citizens. The third war was very brutal and many people try to forget those dark times."

"I am still interested. Please, go ahead, Uncle."

"When I was a young boy, my grandfather told me this story about our ancestor, Legate Pontius Telesinius. He was the general of the Samnite legions in the Social War. It was fought over a hundred years ago between the dictator Sulla and the Roman Populares. The Populares, joined by the Samnites, were fighting to increase social mobility for the lower classes. Telesinius led the army of the Populares in the Battle of Colline Gate, fought just outside the walls of Rome. Before the battle, Telesinius is reported to have said, 'Rome itself must be destroyed, for there would never be an end to wolves preying upon the liberty of Italy, unless the forest in which they took refuge was cut down.' Sulla's army won the battle. Although several thousand Samnites laid down their weapons and surrendered, General Sulla executed them."

"Uncle, what happened to Telesinius?"

"He lay dead among thousands of bodies. Sulla planned to decapitate the dead leaders and catapult their heads over the wall into the city of Praeneste, the last Populares' stronghold. Members of the Pontii family who lived in Rome, unknown to the Pontii of Samnium, risked their lives and slipped onto the battleground where the bodies lay. They removed the body of Telesinius, cremated him, and conveyed his ashes to his family in Samnium. We are descended from them."

Epiphanius asked, "Where are the Pontii who rescued him? Are their descendants still in Rome?"

"I don't know, nephew. We never heard again of the Pontii who recovered Telenisius's body. When I related this story to my father, he seemed irritated and told me to never mention it again. I did not realize why he was so bitter at the time, but now I understand he did not want to relive the Roman persecution of his ancestors.

"I have inherited two animal skins covered with symbols and diagrams from our ancestors. We can study these parchments together later and you can help me figure out their mysteries."

Pilatus looked down at his ring with the red and green garnets. *I wonder if studying the skins would explain the meaning of the gems?* The traffic thinned as they moved farther south along Appian Way. They saw occasional freight wagons and vehicles transporting mail for the Roman state postal service. Although Roman roads were commonplace throughout the empire, no matter how often he traveled upon them, Pilatus still marveled at the engineering. As he rocked side to side upon his mount, images of road building methods rolled through his mind. "Epiphanius, from your studies did you learn about road building?"

"No, I did not study any construction."

"This road is the Appian Way, built over three hundred years ago by the Roman censor, Appius Claudius. Romans build roads in layers. First, a ditch waist deep and twenty paces wide is dug and filled with loose rubble. Layers of sand, stones, and concrete are put down topped by large stones, which are joined by fine limestone concrete to create a smooth surface."

Epiphanius read the engraving at the top of a stone column alongside the road. "$\bar{X}$ MILLE PASSUM – Ten thousand paces. It must mean we have gone ten miles. We are ten miles from Rome."

"You are correct, nephew."

In the evening, the travelers stopped to camp near a grove of ancient chestnut trees. An inn was nearby, but Pilatus suggested they sleep in the fresh air. After they made camp, Pilatus said, "Epiphanius, the Roman legions planted thousands of these chestnuts trees all over Europe. We will make chestnut bread tonight to take advantage of this natural source of food, like the legionaries have done for centuries. See those buildings over there? Here is a silver coin and a handful of bronze coins. Go to the inn and bring back a small jug of ordinary wine. Don't let them convince you to buy the more expensive aged wine. Be careful to go to the taburna, which should be a safe and reputable inn. The other one will be a cheap inn, a caupona, where rough necks and prostitutes consort."

In the twilight, Pilatus followed at a distance as Epiphanius walked to the cluster of buildings. The young man entered the front door of the only building with lights inside. Pilatus slipped in secretly behind him and sat in a dark corner. *The taburna is closed. Nigrinus will be furious if Epiphanius gets hurt, but he said he wanted experiences.* The room was filled with tables peopled by a rowdy and noisy crowd and lit by overhead and wall oil lamps. Epiphanius walked up to the counter to order the wine. A woman with an almost comically painted face approached Epiphanius. "What a nice looking young man! I know what you are looking for."

Epiphanius ignored her and placed a silver coin on the counter and said to the bartender, "A jug of wine, please."

He picked up the wine and started to walk to the door. The woman said, "You want to share that jug, honey? For one more copper, we can drink it upstairs."

"No thanks, ma'am."

The bartender bellowed, "Ma'am? MA'AM? Young patrician, do you know where you are and what she is? Are you lost?"

The patrons were laughing. Startled, Epiphanius stopped. The bartender moved between him and the door. "I heard other coins clinking. One way or another, before you leave, you are going to spend all the money in your pockets."

The large man reached out as if to seize Epiphanius. Pilatus stood, ready to interfere. The man appeared to weigh twice as much as Epiphanius. To everyone's surprise, including Pilatus, Epiphanius put the jug on a table and avoided the bartender's grasp. The bartender said, "This little guy wants to fight!"

The larger man made another attempt to grab Epiphanius, but did not try any punches or vicious moves. He seemed to be entertained. But Epiphanius was not. When he dodged the second lunge by the bartender, he stayed within range and thrust his hand, fingers pressed tightly together in the shape of a knife point, into the larger man's neck. The bartender fell unconscious to the floor.

Pilatus thought he would have to snatch his nephew out the

door to safety, but all the patrons were ecstatic, laughing and clapping. The bartender revived. Pilatus's guards entered, although he and Epiphanius had been gone only a short time. They found everyone in a merry mood. They were both handed a cup as the patrons insisted everyone have wine with them before they left.

They made their way back and the cool air cleared their heads. The sky was brilliant with stars. Pilatus sat next to the campfire and said, "Epiphanius, how did you put that guy out so fast?"

"Well, my Greek tutors not only taught me literature and rhetoric, but one of them knew enough Pankration to teach me some effective moves. Apparently, like he said, a precise knife hand strike to that spot on the neck works very well."

Pilatus said, "I heard the Greeks competed in Pankration at their Olympics. Is it like combining boxing and wrestling?"

"Yes, that's right. I did not learn the full combat, just some of the short cut strikes."

Pilatus laughed as he shelled a pile of chestnuts from their rough outer hulls. "Well, nephew, your knife hand or sword hand, or whatever you call it, worked and with a good ending, without any permanent damage. He rubbed one nut on his nose, and then glanced down at the shiny surface.

Epiphanius laughed. "Uncle, what are you doing? Did you have too much wine?"

Out of habit, Pilatus was repeating an old superstition, and was embarrassed. Then he promptly put the nut in his pocket. "Uh . . . that nut is for good luck."

After roasting the chestnuts, Pilatus prepared the bread by

grinding the chestnut flour and mixing it with wheat flour. Memories of his years as a legionary came flooding back when he smelled the bread baking on the open fire. Later the group slept beneath the stars. The air was cool but comfortable if wrapped in a blanket. Epiphanius and Pilatus lay on their backs, the dark sky above brilliant with the stars. Epiphanius talked about his latest theory. "Uncle, had they been contemporaries, who would have won in battle? Who was the best general? Alexander, Julius Caesar, Hannibal, Epirus, Scipio?"

Pilatus was too tired to answer and Epiphanius continued. "Hannibal took advantage of his opponent's strengths and weaknesses. Scipio studied Hannibal's methods, did not fall for his tactics, and defeated him. Epirus won battles all over the Mediterranean." As he went on, no one had to answer or comment. Epiphanius could carry on a one-way conversation all night.

The multitude of stars reminded Pilatus of the times as a boy when he would steal out of the house with his friends. *After a night of cavorting around, we would lay exhausted outdoors, as we gazed at the stars. I would try to count the stars and end up feeling overwhelmed, and could not comprehend the expanse of the stars. This used to scare me, but I can't remember when this feeling stopped.*

5 THE MEETING

Although Metellanus had advised her to take a litter, Procula insisted they walk to her friend's house, where the meeting about the teachings of Jesus would be held. To be modest, she wore her hair in a bun and a simple dress under a light cloak, which she draped over her head as a veil. It was early morning, almost at the second hour of the day, according to the sundial. The meetings were always early on the seventh day of the week, Saturn's Day. Two slaves walked ahead, which cleared a path for Valeria and Procula, as Metellanus followed.

"I look forward to these meetings", said Procula. "It is refreshing to talk of forgiveness and love instead of the gossip I have had to endure around the patrician women. Then at the theater, I overhear the men discuss the gory details of gladiator contests and dog fights."

Valeria nodded and said, "Domina, out of respect, your servants do not speak of the ghastly matches in your presence, but I hear those topics every day in the household."

After walking four blocks, they arrived at the house. The empty litters parked in the front did not surprise Procula. She knew women from wealthy families who had attended the sessions. But one litter parked amid Praetorian guards caught her attention. "Valeria, it can't be! That is the emperor's litter!"

The watchman escorted them inside the house. Metellanus signaled for Procula's slaves to wait outside as he followed Valeria and Procula. Procula hugged the hostess, a friend with whom she had become close since their introduction at one meeting. The hostess said, "Procula, please meet my friends, Priscilla and her husband Aquila. The meeting will be at their house next week."

After a warm exchange of greetings, Procula and Valeria headed to the peristylium. Procula said, "Hmm. Priscilla and Aquila. They were pleasant. Didn't you think their faces were beaming with joy?"

Then Procula whispered to Valeria, "Pilatus knows I attend religious meetings, but I could never have one at my house. And do not discuss it with any of the household."

"Of course, Domina."

As Procula walked into the vestibule, she discovered why the special litter was out front. Drusilla joined them. "Procula, dear, I was sure you would be here after our little talk the other night at the dinner party. Please sit with me so you can explain the rites of Jesus."

Procula's dislike for Drusilla surfaced in her thoughts, and just as fast melted away, when she looked around and remembered that Jesus taught to forgive. *Surrounded by these people, I am compelled to forgive. And Drusilla might be genuinely interested.*

There were thirty to forty people in the courtyard garden, standing, seated on the stone benches, and sitting on the floor. Several children were among them. Procula described the ritual as she sat with Drusilla and Valeria.

"Drusilla, a prayer, called Pater Noster, is recited by everyone in concert, at the beginning and end of the meeting. A follower of Christos Jesus should recite the Pater Noster three times a day. When I first attended, we said the prayer in Greek, but now less educated people attend and the prayer is recited in Latin."

Drusilla whispered, "Please forgive me but I heard rumors that people at these rituals ate flesh and drank blood. Will that happen?"

"No, no! What you heard was a twisted story of a wonderful sacrament called the communio. Jesus died for us. The bread and wine consumed are symbols of the sacrifice of his body. But to take part in communio, one must be baptized. This washes away your sins."

The hostess began the prayer and then most of the people joined in: "Pater noster, qui es incaelis, our Father in heaven . . . et ne nos inducas in tentationem, sed libera nos a malo, and lead us not into temptation, but deliver us from evil. Amen."

The hostess continued, "Please welcome Deaconess Priscilla. The next meeting will be at her house."

Priscilla took the host's place in front of the assembly. "The prayer we recited is a gift from Jesus. When his disciples asked Jesus how to pray, he taught them this prayer. Note that the invocation begins with 'Our Father' and follows with words such as 'deliver us' . . . The prayer is for all of us. We are all God's children.

"Jesus said everyone is equal in God's eyes. The idea that slaves, plebeians, and patricians are equal is an alien concept to Romans. But look around, people from all parts of society are here. This is what Jesus wanted. Please, speak or ask questions."

A man stood to talk. Drusilla whispered to Procula, "He is a senator. I noticed she did not introduce him by his title."

Procula answered, "They avoid pointing out class distinctions."

The senator spoke with an educated Latin accent. After him a freedman spoke in vulgar Latin, and although he did not possess the eloquence of the senator, he was given the same respect. Procula glanced sideways at Drusilla and was pleased. Her new friend remained attentive and did not look judgmental.

At the end of every meeting the communio was conducted. Priscilla and Aquila distributed bread. The couple then administered wine to the believers as they said, "Hoc est enim corpus meum, for this is my body, hic est enim sanguinis mei, for this is my blood."

Following the communio, most of the people departed the meeting. Procula and Drusilla stayed and chatted with the hostess. Drusilla asked, "Procula, how does one become a follower of Jesus?"

"You must make a sincere pledge that you accept Christos as your savior. Then the deacon will baptize you. The third ritual is to take part in the communio."

"I saw some people take the bread with them when they left. Are they poor?" Drusilla said.

"No, they were taking the sacred bread to those believers that could not attend the meeting."

Procula was distracted by a brisk discussion between a middle-aged woman and a young woman in her early teens. She overheard the older woman say, "Please Arena, the meeting is over and we must go home. Antonius looks forward to coming home every day to see you. He'll be waiting now."

The young woman sobbed, "I can't leave, I don't feel well."

The woman said, "Let us go now. We can stop and buy belladonna herb and make tea at home. That will make you feel better. Antonius and I are so happy you are now part of our family."

The teenager became visibly distraught and screamed, "Family? My family is all dead! Those thieves and bastards killed them! I am glad I sent the Praetorians to kill them!"

Drusilla attempted a nurturing attitude that surprised Procula as she went over to the pair. "Ladies, can we help you?"

"Thank you for asking, mistress. I am Livia. My daughter Arena is having her menses." Livia looked at the hostess. "Do you have any wool rolls for her?"

Livia and Arena followed the hostess into a room bordering the courtyard and returned within a few minutes. Arena appeared calmer.

Procula guessed the women were plebeians. Their clothes were clean, however, and they did not look like many of the unfortunate poor who lived in the insulae. The hostess had cups of diluted wine brought as they sat together at a table in the courtyard. Procula said, "Livia and Arena, we are so glad you came to the assembly. Is this your first time here?"

Livia answered, "Ladies, you are so generous, perhaps we should not stay and bother you."

The hostess said, "No, this will be great enjoyment. Just like Jesus said, we should all associate together. And not just when we are praying. Your daughter is pretty. Is she trying a new hair fashion? I like it. Arena, at which bath did you get it styled?"

Livia said, "Mistress, we are simple people. I do not think we can entertain you with our conversation. Are we amusing to you, mistress?"

"No, no, no, I am sorry, I was trying to chat. You must believe me. Arena's hair is very nice! Is it easy to manage?"

Livia appeared to relax. "Well, it was too short to curl, so I added a little henna and attractive hair clips. Until several days ago, we thought Arena was a boy named Arenus! My husband, Antonius, a Vigile, rescued her at the Subura fire. We are so fortunate to have her. He was . . . she was so dirty. On the way to the baths, she told me the truth."

Procula said, "My husband mentioned how Antonius had taken home a boy he rescued. Nigrinus and Pilatus speak highly of your husband, Livia."

Drusilla asked Arena, "So where are you from, do you remember your family?"

Livia added, "Arena has not spoken much with me. She is recovering from her ordeal. Her outburst surprised me."

Arena looked more composed. "Livia, you are kind and so are the ladies. I am . . . remembering things. It's, it's like a flood of memories are coming back. I am feeling better now and so sorry for my behavior. Antonius and Livia have made me happy. It reminds me of the times when I used to play in the street near our house. My father pushed his cart home every day after he sold fruit and vegetables around the city, and then the family would eat meals together, just like at Livia's house. But my mother and father have been dead for years."

Livia asked, "What do you remember about your mother?"

"My mother and I always went to the baths together, just like you and I did yesterday. She also would fix my hair. It was longer then. She told me that before I was born, her parents had owned a store that sold food and wine and Father's parents had even owned vineyards, but the family lost all of it."

Drusilla said, "Arena, it must be comforting that you can recall those memories. I see you have a bulla; does it contain a memento?"

A look of alarm crossed Arena's face as she placed her hand protectively over her heart where her bulla hung. She said, "It was something . . . something that my father gave me."

Drusilla said, "I am sorry, Arena. My childhood was not a happy one. Both my parents died when I was young. Slaves raised me in Tiberius's household and did not rear me in a traditional way. I never had a bulla in my childhood."

After pleasant farewells, Procula thought about the meeting as she walked home. *Drusilla was curious about Jesus's teachings, and that brought us together. She is still a person who deserves respect. I hope Drusilla and Livia can both become my friends.*

6 BENEVENTUM

Pilatus's first stop in Samnium was the town of Caudium, the home of his late parents. Except for his great uncle and aunt, most of the Pontii had moved to Beneventum. His great aunt welcomed them with a refreshing meal and his uncle served their homemade wine. After a visit that seemed too short, they continued for several more hours to the commercial city of Beneventum. Although their arrival was unexpected and Pilatus had not seen his cousins since his marriage ceremony ten years earlier, he was warmly welcomed.

Several of his cousins, siblings Lucius, Maria, and Nuncia, were eager to guide Pilatus and Epiphanius around their city. They were friendly and gracious as well as highly educated, having been tutored by Greek scholars in Capua. At each relative's home, they enjoyed delicious food and local specialties. Their relatives insisted they have more food even when they had eaten their fill.

One evening they were relaxing in the courtyard of their cousins' house, sipping on wine. Epiphanius asked, "Your city's name literally means 'good wind.' Is that why it is named Beneventum, because you get sweet breezes here?"

Nuncia laughed. "Not exactly! In ancient times herdsmen drove swine across the river at the ford. Because of the odors associated with the hogs, the Samnites named the town Maleventum, or bad wind."

As they laughed, Nuncia continued, "Our grandfather told us that when Roman colonists came to the city hundreds of years ago, they changed the name to Beneventum due to superstition."

Lucius said, "There is another story about the name."

Maria interjected, "Oh no, he is always making jokes. What is he going to say now?"

Lucius continued, "The place derived the name Maleventum from a tribe of people who lived here long before the Samnites. They were mad people that had a wind storm inside their head. The name meant 'a place of crazy people.'"

"Yes, and Lucius is one of their descendants!" Maria said.

After their laughter quieted, Pilatus showed his hosts the animal skin he had inherited from his ancestors. His cousins were intrigued.

After viewing the skin and its symbols, Lucius said, "Uncle, our grandfather told us when he was young his family had lived in a mountain village named Cominium. They had moved far into the mountains to flee Sulla's men who were driving Samnites from their homes. After the violence and chaos settled, his family came out of hiding and returned to Beneventum. They blended in with the Roman colonists and avoided further persecution. I am thankful that is past and we are now protected by law as Roman citizens."

Nuncia added, "Then several years ago, an old man named Pontius Marianus arrived in Beneventum looking for his son

Cominius. He was from the same village that Grandfather remembered. But none of us knew of his son. He showed us a skin like this one."

"When the old man decided to go back to his village, he appeared fragile, so I escorted him," Lucius said. "From the base of the mountain where he lived, he headed for a rocky outcropping, but insisted I not follow him. We never heard of him again."

Pilatus said, "I want to talk to him. Lucius, can you show the way?"

"Yes, I can find the rocky escarpment, then from there we can search for his village."

Within several days, their mounted party departed along unpaved roads. Pilatus's two guards took the vanguard and rearguard as usual. Pilatus wanted to make a good impression and had brought along two burros loaded with gifts. Among the items was an amphora of wine, fruit, and olive oil, products that he knew were not easily available in the mountains. Eventually the roads ended and gave way to narrow mountain trails. These single-tracks were part of the network of sheep and goat trails that crisscrossed the Apennine Mountains. They had evolved from ancient, natural paths created by the movements of wild herds that had traversed the mountains.

Not until Pilatus escaped the bustling noise and activity of the city did he relax. *For once, Epiphanius is quiet. He has exhausted himself talking with his cousins.* The only sounds now were those of the saddles creaking, horses breathing and the plodding of their hooves. He suddenly experienced a yearning to explore the hills and mountains, recognizing them as his homeland. *These trails take a meandering and circuitous route as they follow the terrain. The wild animals that created this trail and* the sheep and goats that followed have taken the path of least resistance. *In contrast, the first part of my journey was on the obsessively straight Roman roads. The 'straight' Roman way is the discipline of hard work, efficiency, and impartial justice. I was raised that way and it was reinforced during my twenty years in the legions. But . . . I did not maintain the Roman discipline with 'him.'*

Dark thoughts haunted him again as they had for over three years. *My schemes did not work. He did not utter one word to Harod. The king thought he was a joke and sent him back. Then, I never thought they would pick Barabbas. Jesus did want to be martyred. That is why he did not defend himself. But why did he talk to me at all when he could see I wanted to release him? And even in crisis, I sensed he pitied me. His eyes. He was not a fanatic, he controlled the situation. Why me? Why was I part of that tragedy?*

The horse stumbled, startling Pilatus from his reverie. He shook his head, trying to rid his mind of the disturbing thoughts. There had been many crises in his life and he had made thousands of judgments during his time as Prefect of Judea. Throughout his career he had not regretted any of his decisions, until this one.

At midday, the party rode up a steep track. They stopped to rest along the trail as Pilatus and Epiphanius inspected carvings and inscriptions on the rocky walls. Lucius joined them, "Relics and inscriptions like these are common along these wilderness trails."

"Are these pictures of gods?" Epiphanius asked.

Nuncia answered, "The relief figures are shepherds. Yes, they are revered, but not as deities. In old times, goat and sheep farming was a sacred ritual due to its relation to the seasonal movements of the ancient herds. The shepherds were a hardy folk and disappeared with their flocks for months into the high rugged mountains. They endured severe weather and deprivations. These shepherds were wise men and were called priests."

Pilatus said, "So, they worshiped their shepherd ancestors, similar to the Romans' custom of worshiping their forebears. I have a niche in my house, and so do you, Epiphanius, with a statue, the family's Lars Familiaris representing an ancient ancestor. The tradition starts with the relationships we have with our parents and grandparents, whose spirits stay with us after they pass away."

The group was quiet. Pilatus continued, "When I was a boy near Caudium, I was a shepherd, but it was much tamer than the conditions the ancients experienced. I remember we had the lower meadows in the winter and moved the herds into the high meadows in the summer."

Epiphanius pointed to the top of a nearby ridge. "Are those ruins of a stone watchtower?"

Lucius said, "Yes. Long before Samnium became part of Rome, the Samnites had built strongholds on the mountain ridges. They overlooked the sheep tracks and river valleys and allowed them to control these natural roads. This trail will lead us to Cominium, which I am guessing was one such stronghold."

Epiphanius said, "Where did you learn so much about Samnite history?"

"My sisters and I first learned from Greek tutors in Capua. They stimulated us to ask questions about everything. So, when we returned to Beneventum, we asked our elders."

"We should record this information and the stories about the family." said Epiphanius.

After traveling another hour the trail reached its highest point, and they entered a flat grassy meadow several hundred paces wide, occupied by goats. A massive rock face rose above the far side of the meadow. The rock had been hollowed out, and included windows and doors, which had transformed it into what appeared to be a three-story building. Embrasures had been carved at the top making the structure look like a fortification. Several stone houses and huts were at the base of the cliff.

Two elderly women and an old man with a long white beard approached the mounted visitors. Suddenly, a young man in his teens, who had been shielded in the tall grass, emerged among the goats and joined the threesome. The elderly man put his arm around the young man's shoulders. Both wore identical amulets around their necks and metal bands wrapped around their wrists and up the forearms. They walked calmly, each with a shepherd's short staff, a bastonem. The older man smiled and said, "Are you lost?"

Pilatus said, "Sir, we are looking for Pontius Marianus." The young man appeared surprised and looked at the white-haired man. Pilatus dismounted.

The elder said, "You are looking for me I suppose. I am Pontius Marianus. This young shepherd, my grandson, is . . . also Marianus."

"Do you remember these young people from Beneventum?", asked Pilatus.

"Yes, but, we were expecting you, too, my son."

7 COMINIUM

Pilatus proposed to Epiphanius that he return to Beneventum with his cousins. His nephew, excited to experience more of their lifestyle and culture, approved. One of the guards went with Epiphanius. Pilatus kept the other guard with him in Cominium. There he could concentrate on the family relics and continue dialogues with the elder Marianus.

The next morning, Pilatus joined Marianus and his grandson after they returned from the meadows tending the goats. They sat outside the immense rock house on benches next to a weather-beaten table. An elderly woman brought bread, goat cheese, and bowls of nuts. Pilatus smiled at the woman, "Thank you. This chestnut bread is delicious, just how I like it, and I haven't had pistachio nuts since I was a youngster."

The woman smiled and returned to sit in the shade with her companion. Pilatus thought, *"This is amusing. There are four inhabitants of this village, two old ladies and two Marianii."*

The elder Marianus said, "All these nuts and the cranberries grow nearby."

"Who are the two ladies? Do they make this wonderful cheese?"

"Oh, they say they are my cousins, but they are just slaves. Yes, yes, it is good cheese."

The young man interjected, "Papa! You are being mean again! Pilatus, they are . . . our servants. Our real cousins and family left years ago. My parents remained, making a living by shepherding. Then when I was little, Papa said it was when I was five, they drove a herd of cattle down toward Beneventum and never returned. Papa and I have, er . . . and the ladies, have taken care of each other since then."

Pilatus said, "I am sorry your parents did not return."

"It is sad. I think thieves killed my parents. That was over ten years ago. As I grew up, Papa taught me how to be a shepherd, including how to use the sling and the bastonem."

The young man beamed at his grandfather and said, "We are good partners."

He then whispered, "Papa thinks you are his son, Cominius, who has returned. But you have seen how his mind lapses."

"His son's name was Cominius? Hmmm. Cominium. Based on the abandoned houses, it looks like there may have been scores of people living here . . . but a long time ago. Perhaps the village was named after one of your ancestors."

"Sir . . . , Pilatus . . . cousin . . . , what should I call you?"

"Older male cousins may be called Uncle."

"Yes, Uncle. Papa has told me many interesting stories. Although he has problems with his daily memory, he remembers events from long ago. Papa! Tell us the story about the Lover of the Sea . . . about Pontus."

Pilatus said, "Pontus, the province in Asia?

"Um . . . I am not sure what you mean, Uncle."

"Maybe you mean sea, as in the inland sea, Pontus Euxinus, also called the Black Sea?"

"Yes, it is about a sea. I have never seen one, but Papa says a sea is like a spring lake so wide you cannot see to the other side. I think that is amazing!"

Pilatus said, "That is a good description."

The grandfather began his story, "The goddess Gaia, the great mother of all, gave birth to a water god named Pontus. Being a minor god, his realm was only a large lake. But Pontus was jealous of Oceanus, the god of the oceans. He planned to steal water from Oceanus's dominion. This would create a great flood, so Pontus warned a worthy man, who was the leader of a village which had been built upon platforms in the shallows of the lake. Then, Pontus created earthquakes that cracked the land between the lake and the Mediterranean Sea. Floodwaters roared into the lake for many days. As the water level increased and threatened to flood their houses, the lake dwellers cut their platforms free of their pilings. People, animals, the entire village floated atop the floodwaters. The wind and currents carried them south. Days later they arrived at the shore of the enlarged lake, now a sea connected to the Mediterranean. The leader became a devoted follower of Pontus and was afterwards known as – Lover of Pontus, Lover of the Sea."

Day after day the elder told stories that intrigued Pilatus. Then one day Pilatus saw the two shepherds – grandfather and grandson – sparring with their bastoni. He had learned the staff when he was a young shepherd in Samnium. Then he had moved to Rome to be educated and lived with Nigrinus's family. The staffs were used as walking sticks and were also utilized as bludgeons against wolves and other threats to the herds. The two circled each other and twirled their staves high, which formed a moving umbrella as defense against their opponent's attack. If one competitor went on the offense, the other would divert their rotating staff to intercept and counterattack.

They stopped their friendly contest. Marianus said, "Uncle, do you want to spar?"

Pilatus, interested, joined them and asked the elder Marianus, "May I borrow your bastonem, sir?"

He stepped back dramatically, whipped his staff overhead in a series of loops, and said, "Please, use my grandson's staff."

The young man smiled, handed his staff to Pilatus and said, "He is unpredictable. Good luck."

Pilatus began with caution. *I do not want to hurt the old man. It has been forty years since I last picked up a bastonem! Its style of fighting is unlike the Roman sword which I used in battle for decades. A Roman short sword, hardly longer than my forearm, is held by one hand to thrust. This lengthier bastonem is wielded with both hands, and like a two-handed sword is used to sweep with wide arcs.*

They circled each other. Pilatus copied Marianus as he twirled his staff overhead and around his body. Multiple times after a flurry of strikes and blocks, the older man's staff ended up stinging Pilatus's wrist or hand. They would stop, break apart and resume. Pilatus decided to score a few points of his own. He pressed his attacks. He scored a hit, but Grandfather answered with several in retaliation. The elder Marianus dropped his guard and said, "That's enough for an old man. That was exciting, Cominius!"

Pilatus did not have the heart to correct him. "Well done, Papa!"

#

Several days later the grandfather and Pilatus sat in the sun sharing food and wine. Young Marianus had returned after retrieving a few goats that had wandered away. He said, "Papa, do you have a new tale for us?"

His grandfather said, "You look familiar, young man. What is your name?"

"Uh . . . it's Marianus, the same as your name, Papa."

Pilatus placed his animal skins on the table and asked the elder Marianus, "Papa, you told us the story about the man who became 'Lover of Pontus.' That story must describe how the Black Sea formed. Do you know any more stories of him after he came ashore? In this area on the map – in Asia? See these green dots in a line across Asia?"

The elder man traced the green dotted line with his finger from the south shore of the Black Sea and stopped on the west coast of Asia Minor on the Aegean Sea.

Pilatus said, "Yes, that is Troy. Did Lover of Pontus go there?"

The elder Marianus stuttered and stopped.

Young Marianus and Pilatus waited for Papa to continue. Pilatus asked, "Lover of Pontus went to Troy?"

The elder Marianus asked his grandson, "What is your name, you look familiar."

The young man had a tear on his cheek as he held a bowl of

olives for his grandfather and said, "I am Marianus, Papa. Have some of these beautiful olives that Pilatus brought for us!"

The grandfather drank wine and ate a few olives, but then was as quiet and motionless as a statue. His hands with wrinkled skin were folded upon the old gray table, its cracks and split grains showing its many years as well.

Pilatus said, "You are a good grandson, Marianus. Let Papa rest and we will spar for a while." Pilatus looked down at the bruises young Marianus had inflicted on his arms from an earlier match. "I bet I will outscore you today!"

As they circled each other, their attention was diverted by a figure on horseback crossing the meadow. Lucius had arrived. Marianus was ready to barrage Lucius with a thousand questions about Beneventum, Capua, and the outside world.

Lucius dismounted his horse and handed Pilatus a leather tube marked with the emblem of the imperial express postal service. He said, "Uncle, this arrived in Beneventum yesterday."

Pilatus feared the letter was a directive from Caligula. He opened the leather cylinder and pulled out a papyrus scroll. When he saw his cousin Nigrinus's seal affixed to the scroll, he was relieved. The letter was in Procula's handwriting:

You know that you are the whole world and nothing else matters. Before you read the rest of this letter, know that I am safe and in good health. Do not think about rushing back to Rome. Our future depends on you remaining in Samnium until Caligula calls for you. Trust me. I have discussed this with Nigrinus. He agrees and I know you respect his judgment.

Pilatus's first urge was to read the rest of the letter, but he needed to be alone now. "Excuse me, cousin Lucius."

#

Pilatus sat on a bench in the dimly lit room of the rock house, with his scrolls and books spread out on the table. Although there were several small windows, most of the light was provided from the ceiling skylight by polished metal reflectors. Pausing, transfixed by the shaft of light, he realized he had never paid attention to this marvel. He turned his attention back to the letter.

My husband, life in the city for the average citizen goes on as usual. But for the patricians and equestrians, Caligula's reign has created a pall of fear and horror. Many people knew Caligula was immoral and cruel. As entertainment, Caligula recited stories of Mars, Mercury, and Jupiter swooping down from Olympus and raping mortal women. Claiming his right as a god, Caligula had stopped in villages as he returned from his campaigns in the north and had randomly raped innocent women. It was well known he was having affairs with many of the senators' wives, but now his behavior has taken a more perverse turn.

During a recent banquet, he retired to his bedchambers with Senator Silvius's wife. While we were still having dinner, Caligula walked out with Silvius's wife and went on about her sexual capacity and her attributes. Silvius showed extreme control at this, although the veins bulged in his neck. He saved his life by joining with the guests in an ovation for Caligula with the guests. It was the only action that would satisfy Caligula after the awkward silence that followed his lewd description of the encounter.

Caligula then pointed at Macro and accused him of prostituting his wife to him. As punishment, Caligula gave Macro two choices. He could either take solitary exile, which would mean all his family's property would be confiscated, or commit suicide, which by law, would ensure his family would inherit his estate.

The next day Macro, your friend, died by his own hand. What an ironic outcome for the Praetorian who put Caligula in power. Caligula must have paid the Praetorians extravagant amounts in bribes.

Pilatus's heart raced and beads of sweat formed on his forehead as he continued to read, anxious as to what he would discover next.

Since this horrible event I have made various excuses, no longer accepting invitations to Caligula's gatherings. Nigrinus has sent several of his own guards to our house to reinforce Metellanus and the doorman. Metellanus assembled our slaves and ordered them not to reveal any details about our house or number of guards to anyone. Metellanus has supplied the house with enough daggers to arm all the slaves. He says we should not expect to see Praetorians knocking on the door, but instead expect an assault by hired hoodlums so it would appear that Caligula was not involved.

Drusilla knows her brother Caligula better than anyone and she says I must beware. You may wonder why she cares. She has joined me at the prayer meetings and is now my close friend. I believe God has sent her to help me. With Drusilla's friendship, I am safe.

Do not return to Rome until Caligula sends for you. We will be together soon. I am praying for us. Love, Procula.

8 THE LAST FIRE

Arena had just returned from the baths with Livia and was looking forward to Antonius returning home from his work. *This is what happiness feels like! Life can be good! What a wonderful feeling! I used to be hungry every day, running and hiding to avoid danger. Then Antonius brought me home. I haven't had a home for years. Yes, home. NOW MY HOME!*

Livia said, "Arena, go to the roof and get enough chickpeas and carrots for a stew."

From the roof garden on the second story, Arena could see Antonius nearing the house. She waved and shouted at him, slid down the ladder to the first-floor roof and ran down the stairs. Arena threw the vegetables on the table and ran through their house out the door. Holding Antonius's hand, she led him into the house, "Antonius is home!"

Antonius laughed, "Livia, why don't you act that way when I come home?"

He wrestled with Arena as Livia said, "Remember, she is not a boy."

Antonius answered out of breath, "But she is tough and quick! Have you seen her run?"

"On second thought, if you wrestle with me, husband, I will give you a cheerful welcome each day!"

Livia cooked the chickpeas into a potage and added carrots. As they sat at the table, she said, "I have figs for later."

Arena's eyes brightened at the thought of the sweet fruit. She spooned stew from her bowl. "Livia, every Saturn's Day for months we have gone to the Christos meetings. They said Jesus wanted us to love all people and trust God because he was in control. And if you believed that Jesus was God's son, you would live an afterlife of joy."

Livia smiled. "Arena, what a good memory. You were listening!"

Arena continued, "At first, I could not believe what the people were saying at the meetings. I looked around and wondered how the other people could believe it. But then Antonius also came and I watched both of your expressions during the meetings. You believe what they say. And now I believe Jesus led Antonius to rescue me. I want to accept Jesus."

"That is wonderful, dear. So, at the next meeting the deaconess will baptize you."

Arena picked up a piece of dark flatbread. "How is the baptism done?"

"Procula said that in Judea she had seen people baptized in a river. They dunked the people under water, but here . . . "

Arena spit some food out as she said, "What?"

Antonius said, "Yes, they hold you under the water until you can't blow anymore bubbles. It's scary!"

"Stop, Antonius!" said Livia. "Don't frighten Arena. The deacon merely splashed water on my head when I was baptized."

There was a knock on the door, and Antonius answered. It was a Vigile calling him to a fire. Livia said, "But you had training all day long! And . . ." Antonius looked at the floor, ready to endure her distress, but she stopped.

Livia picked up a handful of figs and said, "Antonius, be careful. I love you. Take these with you for energy and wake me up when you get home."

Antonius kissed Livia, hugged Arena and kissed her on the cheek. As he exited the house, he called out his customary goodbye, "Livia, Arena, I love you."

Livia retired early. Arena lingered until she was asleep. She removed the hair pins and tousled up her hair to help her assume the role of a street orphan. She stole out of the house and reasoned, *What if the hoodlums attack again? The last time I had to call the Praetorians.*

She located the fire and watched from a distance as Antonius worked with his men, coaxing people to jump out of smoking windows. Visible in a fifth story window were the faces of several children. The Vigiles shouted and gestured, but could not convince them to jump. Arena watched as Antonius and a fellow Vigile entered the building.

Within a minute, Arena saw the two men dropping children out the window, one after another. They landed on the sailcloths held taut by the firemen. Antonius and his partner disappeared from the window. Arena became anxious. Her fears subsided when Antonius exited the bottom floor. He stopped and looked back as if waiting for his partner. Arena shouted from afar, "No, Antonius, no!"

Antonius went back into the burning dwelling. Arena ran toward the building as flames engulfed the entire structure. A thunderous noise of cracking and splintering followed as the entire structure collapsed.

Arena stood in the street crying out, "I needed you more!"

There was no time to mourn. A gang of thugs was running toward her. "That's the little bitch who pointed us out to the Praetorians!"

Arena's senses reverted to the days of survival on the streets. She bolted toward the fire, aware these men could run her down in the streets and knowing she had to somehow outmaneuver them. The men halted to avoid running among the firemen. Their pause gave Arena time to dart into the adjoining neighborhood. She ran to the top floor of an insula. *This is the block where the buildings are close together.* After leaping from roof top to roof top, she located the gang of hoodlums and could hear them talking in the street. "Damn, we may have lost that urchin, but he was with that Vigiles centurion who went berserk at the Palatine fire. I know where he lives. Let's go."

Arena panicked. *Livia!* She ran and jumped to the next rooftop. Continuing to run along the roofs from one building to the next, she tried to reconstruct an image of the neighborhood. *When do the tall buildings end?* Landing on another roof and finding that the roofs were getting farther apart, she increased her speed for the next leap. Arena could hear the wind whistling in her ears. *I barely made that one!* She screamed in her mind. *I will not cry. I will not quit!*

Arena vaulted to another roof, but her tired legs crumbled, and she was pitched forward and hit her head on the roof. Eyes wide open, laying on her back, she saw a bright light. *No! Have I been asleep?* She jumped to her feet. *The moon is up!*

She began her run to the next roof, but slid to a stop. The roof of the next building was far below. The blocks of insula had ended. *I wouldn't have seen that edge without the moon's light. Jesus is lighting the way to save Livia.* Arena raced down to the street.

#

Procula sat in the garden with her friend. "Claudia, dear, it's so wonderful having you here!"

Procula's attendant Valeria filled their cups halfway with red wine. She held a pitcher of water, but Claudia covered her cup. "Valeria, I will have the wine without water. I am that distraught today!"

"I am so sorry, mistress. Do you want belladonna tea?"

"No, no, just more wine."

"Procula, you are so very gracious to let me stay. My husband is still in Mediolanum recruiting new Praetorians. If I had gone home, one of our servants would have told him of the bruises on my arms and face."

Claudia hugged Procula and continued, "You are so kind, not asking me details, but I must talk about it. I was so naive. A message was delivered affixed with Drusilla's seal, inviting me to their villa. She was not even there!"

Claudia sobbed as she said, "Caligula forced himself on me!"

She consumed all her wine in one draft. "I resisted, and that is why he hurt me, but I knew it was no use. If Chaerea finds out, my god . . . I know him. He'll lose his temper and Caligula will murder both of us!"

"Don't worry, dear. Your bruises will heal well before Chaerea returns. He will never know. You are safe here."

Claudia said, "Thank you Procula. I see you have others visiting. May I meet them?"

"Yes, you will meet Livia and her daughter Arena at dinner. They are charming women. Several days ago, Livia's husband Antonius was killed in a fire when a building collapsed. What a horrible tragedy! It makes my heart so heavy for Livia and Arena. The collapse occurred after he had saved the lives of several children and a fellow fireman. Today the bulletin in the forum proclaimed Antonius a hero, and a plaque will be placed on the market wall in his honor. His death, however, is not why Livia and Arena are here. Both are here for protection from hoodlums. They were hunting Arena because she had identified their gang to the Praetorian Guards.

"Let's make something good out of your visit. We can enjoy the company of Livia and the young woman. You will not need to worry. Our house is as secure as a small fortress. Before Pilatus left he ensured there was a formidable complement of guards led by Metellanus. In addition, our guard dog Rusticus will not allow any stranger through the front door."

Later that afternoon, the doorman informed Procula that Drusilla was waiting in the atrium to see her. Procula met her in the study, to avoid alarming Claudia. Drusilla's skin had a sickly pallor. "Drusilla, what brings you here? And why weren't you at the prayer meeting yesterday?"

"I have been sick. I am sorry for poor Claudia. It is sad, but she saved her husband's life when she fought back against Caligula, so he will not punish Chaerea. However, because Macro's wife did not resist my brother, in Caligula's mind, she had no morals. What does my brother know about morals? His mind is contorted. Macro's death was a tragedy.

"I have warned you before of my brother, Procula. Caligula is insane with lust for you. You must never come to our house. Even Nigrinus cannot protect you. My brother is lascivious and plans to sleep with every woman he desires. I know my brother. He has not been able to trap you and thinks if Pilatus were dead, you would submit to him. I think he has plans to execute Pilatus, then destroy your whole family. I have convinced my brother to call Pilatus back to Rome. He must invoke the ancient tradition of suicide, sua manus, at Caligula's command. Then by tradition, your household will be inviolate. Although the Praetorians will stay loyal to Caligula, sua manus is such a strong custom that the Praetorian Guard will not harm you."

Procula could not believe what she was hearing. She said, "No, no! I will tell Pilatus, no matter what: Do not to return to Rome. It would be better to never see him again."

Drusilla whispered, "Do not fear, my friend, I have a fabulous deception. Pilatus will kneel before Caligula, but hidden in the folds of his toga will be the intestines of a pig, filled with its own blood. Pilatus will plunge his dagger into the lining, releasing what appears to be his lifeblood, thus convincing Caligula he has disemboweled himself. I will arrange for my most loyal slaves to remove his body, when Caligula is distracted. Coordinate with Pilatus as soon as he is called back to Rome. I recommend arranging a secret location in the provinces where you can both flee afterwards and live in exile."

As Drusilla said these last words, Procula was already composing the letter she would send to Pilatus.

9 RETURN TO ROME

Papa had been silent for several days, ever since he had stopped in mid-sentence telling a story about Troy. This morning, however, he had woken up very animated and would not stop talking. He had called for bread, cheese, wine mixed with honey, and goat's milk. The two women had graciously brought the food. Pilatus and the younger Marianus were surprised when Papa asked the women to stay and eat with them. They had seemed pleased but did not enter the conversations. After the meal, he had insisted the three men walk together in the meadows and check on the goats.

As they surveyed the goat herd, the elder Marianus said, "Grandson, I see you have castrated this spring's young males. That is good for the herd. We do not need any bucklings interfering with our two healthy bucks. I do need you to repair the head catch on the milking stand. And help the women when they milk the goats by filling the stand's feed buckets. Also, they are almost out of rennet for their cheese. There is a patch of artichoke thistle near the creek. They cannot walk well anymore, so please bring them five bundles before this evening."

He addressed Pilatus, "Cominius, thank you for going to town and bringing back the supplies. We can talk later about the money you got for the cattle."

They returned to the weathered table where they had spent hours eating, studying the old skins, and telling stories. Lying across the table was a bastonem made of dark olive wood. The curvilinear staff gave Pilatus the impression of a black snake ready to strike. A knob on one end created an ideal place for a tight grip.

"Grandson, I can still detect when you are going to attack with your staff. Keep the movement of the bastonem smoother through the change in direction. Cominius, you are improving daily. Keep up your shadow practice. You are getting better," the elder Marianus said.

Papa picked up the dark bastonem and threw it to Pilatus as he shouted, "Cominius, your new bastonem has a name. It is called L'Olivastro. Protect yourself!"

Grandfather and grandson, Marianus and Marianus, circled Pilatus. They moved in the style that the shepherds called 'walking the circle.' Pilatus began his own pattern trying to prevent them from surrounding him. *I feel like I am being stalked by wolves, the ultimate challenge of the shepherd.*

Pilatus reacted and countered their attacks. He did not remember how long their mock combat lasted nor any details of the flurry of their movements. But grandfather and grandson must have been satisfied with Pilatus's performance because they terminated the combat. He leaned over, out of breath. His two comrades were weary as well.

They retired to the familiar table and quenched their thirst with diluted wine. Papa said, "I have done everything I wanted to do today. In fact, I have done everything I wanted to do my whole life. The goats, the food, the family, the bastoni play. I am happy! Oh, there is one more undone task – After Pontus arrived in Troy, he married a Trojan woman and raised a family. His descendants fled with Aeneas to Italy. But there was a stop at an island . . ." Papa took a sip of wine and slumped over on the table.

#

The women prepared Papa's body for burial. The Samnites ritual included burying their dead, unlike the Roman tradition of cremation followed by interment of the ashes. Papa's beloved bastonem was buried with him.

In the days following the grandfather's passing, Marianus had found it difficult to overcome his sorrow. He appeared unhappy even when he led the goats to pasture. Pilatus began accompanying him and he improved marginally. When Pilatus told Marianus he would teach him how to read, using the stories his grandfather had dictated to him, the young man brightened.

Several days later, while Marianus was moving the goat herd to a higher pasture, his keen eyes detected his cousin Lucius leading a group of soldiers far below along the switchback trails. He could not understand why they were not making much progress toward the village. It appeared Lucius was lost, since he had led the group over the same area three or four times using different routes. Mystified, he ran to the rock house and notified Pilatus. Pilatus, Marianus, and Pilatus's guard watched while Lucius led the small group of Praetorians through the ravines and fields on the narrow trails below.

"Uncle, what is Lucius doing?"

"Son, he is delaying their arrival to give me an opportunity to decide whether I want to see these visitors or flee."

"Those are legionaries!" Marianus exclaimed.

"They are not just Roman legionaries, but they are members of the Praetorian Guard, an elite legion whose duty is to protect the Emperor."

"Why are they here, Uncle?"

Pilatus also wondered why the men were sent. *When Procula had said to wait for Caligula to send for me, I had expected a letter, not this escort — or worse — an arrest by Praetorian Guards. Caligula would not send an assassin squad. If he wanted me killed, his nature would drive him to experience the cruelty firsthand. I trust Procula's advice.*

"Marianus, it is likely I am being summoned by the emperor. And they will escort me. I would like to stay longer, but it is necessary I return to Rome."

I do not want to involve either Lucius or Marianus. I know these Praetorians and they might be receptive to my appeals to let the boy remain here and Lucius to return to his home.

Pilatus assessed the Praetorian squad as they dismounted and paused along the trail on the steep hill. He recognized the Tribune Gaius Chaerea. They had both served on the frontier together and in the Praetorian Guard in Rome. Pilatus stepped out from behind the bushes from where they had observed the Praetorians' approach and waved his arm side to side to gain their attention.

Chaerea shouted from down the hill. "Pontius Pilatus, Caligula orders you to return to Rome."

Other than Macro, he felt he could trust Chaerea better than anyone in the Guard. Pilatus called out, "Gaius Chaerea, come up alone so we can talk face to face."

Lucius stayed with the Praetorian squad as Chaerea hiked up the switchbacks to join Pilatus. As Chaerea talked, Pilatus was reminded that Chaerea's voice was at least an octave higher than that of the average man. Years ago, the pitch of Chaerea's voice had increased after losing a testicle from a battle wound, although it had not affected his ability to father several sons and daughters. Caligula frequently made derogatory remarks about Chaerea's voice and challenged his masculinity.

Pilatus and Chaerea talked out of hearing range of Marianus and Pilatus's bodyguard. Chaerea said, "Friend, it is distressing to tell you that Caligula has changed your punishment from exile to sua manus. If you do not comply, the Pontii clan will lose their homes, livelihood, and perhaps their lives. Procula is waiting for you at the Boar Inn south of Rome."

Pilatus said, "Why would Caligula give me the better option? Perhaps he has sent you here just to kill me?"

Chaerea pulled a leather tube out of his tunic and handed it to Pilatus. As he pulled a scroll out of the cylinder, Pilatus noted a wax seal with the emperor's insignia held the scroll together. He unrolled the document and read Caligula's summons which commanded him to commit suicide. He then noticed a small piece of folded papyrus still in the tube. It was a note in Procula's handwriting. *Come to Rome. Nigrinus says Epiphanius must stay in Samnium. Procula.*

Chaerea said, "Pilatus, I risked my life and my family to put that note in there. Will you come?"

#

Pilatus gathered his belongings. It was difficult to say goodbye. He promised he would return to Cominium, and he hoped the lie would lessen Marianus's grief over Papa's death.

"Son, I will be back within several weeks. Epiphanius would like to come and stay in Cominium a while. What do you say to that?"

Marianus's eyes brightened. "You said he was a scholar. Yes, I will welcome his company. It will be interesting."

Pilatus was encouraged and said, "Teach him the bastonem and you will have a sparring partner. In addition, he will continue your reading lessons."

Pilatus embraced his young cousin goodbye and departed. with the Praetorians. Due to Chaerea's lenience, they stopped in Beneventum where Pilatus gave Epiphanius his father's instructions to stay in Samnium. When he urged Epiphanius to go see Marianus in Cominium, he agreed. Pilatus said Nigrinus would be coming within a fortnight.

As they rode, Pilatus knew he would not be returning and regretted the necessity of the lies to Marianus. *I will be gone, but Nigrinus will welcome Marianus into his family. What it could have been! I would have adopted him. Without thinking, I had been calling Marianus 'son.' It seemed natural.*

#

Just ahead Pilatus could see the Boar Inn, the refreshment house and hotel of the Three Taverns, the last rest stop before Rome along the Appian Way. Built of stone, the three-story inn was stuccoed and painted light orange. Terra cotta tiles covered the roof. A wooden sign hung over the front door with the engraved image of a wild boar.

Chaerea said, "Caligula will expect you tomorrow, so you can rest at the inn tonight. There is a room ready for you."

The innkeeper gave Pilatus his room number on the second

floor. As Pilatus climbed the stairs, each step seemed a tremendous effort. He opened the door and saw Procula. Elated to see her, he forgot about the tiredness, the Praetorians, the journey, or what might happen the next day. Her lips were cool and sweet.

Hours later he awoke. There was a soft glow from the oil lamp on the table next to the bed. He lay on his back and opened his eyes, briefly watching the play of light and shadows on the ceiling. It was quiet, save for the deep breathing of his wife next to him. He was momentarily disoriented. *Am I at home in Rome?* There was a sinking feeling as he recognized he was at the inn. She stirred as Pilatus said, "Procula, it was wonderful, just as it has always been."

Procula smiled sleepily. "Yes, and now I will tell you our plan."

Pilatus raised his eyebrows. "Plan?"

She got out of bed and crossed the room. Even after many years together, Pilatus still admired the gentle curves of her slim body. She put on her robe and handed Pilatus a cup of wine. Her expression transformed from drowsy to focused.

Pilatus sipped wine as Procula repeated Drusilla's plan. "Caligula will want your act to be formal, so it will be natural that you will be wearing a toga. This will make it easy to hide this under your clothes." She held up what looked to be a vest of animal skin. The semi-transparent skin was filled with blood.

"You will wear this lining and puncture it with a thrust from your dagger. The blood will gush out, soak your toga, and give the impression you have inflicted a mortal wound."

Pilatus said, "It's too dangerous. If Caligula suspects anything, everyone suffers. No, I must make this sacrifice."

Procula was silent.

Pilatus added, "Who knows of this plot?"

"Only Drusilla, Chaerea, Nigrinus, and Metallanus."

"Chaerea knows. Yes, he hates Caligula. And Nigrinus agreed. What will he do if it fails?"

"He is committed and is certain it will work. Nigrinus's wife is here at the inn. Tomorrow she will go to Beneventum to join Epiphanius. They will be far from Rome and go into hiding if the plan does not work."

Pilatus said, "No, there is too much risk."

Procula held both of Pilatus's hands as she said, "I will not live without you. You must try this deception. This is our only chance to be together. If you commit suicide, I will do the same."

"Go on with describing the plan," said Pilatus.

"As always, Drusilla will be at Caligula's side. She has arranged a distraction, and she will have slaves remove your body before Caligula has had time to form any suspicions. Metellanus will slip you out of the city and we will meet at my father's estate in the Alps. I have everything ready."

Pilatus examined the liquid-filled lining and put on the vest, yet still looked unconvinced. He took another sip of wine and stared absently. He smiled and said, "Metellanus also predicts it will work? All right, then we will make it work."

Later they lay in bed holding hands; a cool breeze of air entered the window, helping to clear the tension from the room. Pilatus's mind raced and neither could sleep. Procula had never told Pilatus about her prayer meetings and Christ.

"Pilatus, have you ever wondered what I was doing when I went to the prayer meetings?"

She has the courage to bring up a forbidden subject because she does not have to consider my eyes.

An uncomfortable silence followed and Procula ventured, "Have I made you angry?"

Pilatus broke the tension and answered calmly, "No, I imagined you were praying to the Jewish god."

"Yes, but we also pray to his son Christos, who died so we may be freed of our sins. Because of his sacrifice, when our time on earth ends, we will then live in joy in heaven everlasting. I have prayed to Christos that if our plan does not work, your spirit will rise to the stars in Heaven. The only way I can suffer your death is that I know I will join you there someday."

This is not the time to ridicule her faith. It gives her hope and strength. He said, "Go on, I want to hear more."

Procula ardently continued late into the night as Pilatus listened.

10 SUA MANUS

Early the next morning, Praetorian guards escorted Pilatus to his house. He said farewell to the members of his household, and joined Metellanus to share a final cup of wine.

"Thank you a thousand times for keeping Procula safe and for protecting the household."

Pilatus placed a scroll and a leather sack on the table. The pouch resonated with the clink of coins. He raised his cup. "You have been the most loyal bodyguard, a friend, and a comrade. With this wine, I salute you. Freedom and long life! You are now a freedman. Here is your manumission document, and a gift as a token of my appreciation for your service."

Metellanus raised his cup. "Thank you, Pilatus, comrade and friend. You are most generous! But I cannot envision leaving your family. I wish I could take your place today. I wonder . . . In fact . . ."

"Shhhh. No, no. Discard the idea of a double deception. Metellanus, this is my duty. But it is unusual. We look so much alike, yet are from different ends of the world. I was born in southern Italy and you in Caledonia. Do you regret my father taking you from your homeland?"

"No, I had so many older brothers, there was no inheritance left for me. I have had it better here, serving you, instead of living as a poor man in Caledonia. I have had a good life with the Pontii clan. Pilatus, you will find this amusing. While you were exiled in Samnium, Caligula received a report that you were seen in the Forum. Two Praetorian guards arrested me and took me to their commanding officer, Tribune Chaerea. He had a good laugh when he saw it was me detained by two of his men."

They laughed together. Pilatus looked at the sundial. "It is the eighth hour. I am to report to Caligula for the sua manus in one hour. I will not say goodbye."

Pilatus went to his bedroom to prepare. Procula examined his vest filled with blood and made sure it was secure. Pilatus pulled his tunic over the vest. As Procula helped him put on a white toga with purple stripes along the left side, she said, "Metallanus, Nigrinus, and I will be there. Drusilla will be ready. Our plan will work!"

She kissed him and embraced him for a long moment. Procula then stepped back in mock attention, but with tears in her eyes, and pounded her right fist on her chest and said, "Virtus!"

Pilatus returned her salute and they laughed and gained courage together.

#

Just before the ninth hour, Praetorian guards led Pilatus to a large building near the Senate in the Forum. They entered the building and proceeded down a long hallway which was framed by two parallel colonnades. Along the sides of the hall were statues of Roman gods, and on pedestals, busts of Caesar Augustus and Caligula. The sunlight reflected brilliantly off the floor of polished marble. The far end of the hall widened with adjacent wings where scribes, accountants, and magistrates were assembled around desks. Caligula sat upon a white marble curule chair, the traditional seat of Roman law and authority.

Several senators had finished their business with Caligula. They avoided eye contact with Pilatus as they passed and left the building.

Two Praetorian guards accompanied Pilatus as he walked toward Caligula. When the trio came within ten paces of the emperor, they stopped. The guards stepped back a pace, leaving Pilatus standing alone.

Caligula spoke, "Glad to see you back, Pilatus. Did you enjoy your goats?" He laughed. "I knew you would return. I find it amusing you take such pride in the old-fashioned Roman virtues that put family and country first."

Pilatus remained silent. The emperor continued, "Romans honor their family and their gods. You will do both today. And I being a god will likewise honor the ancient Roman traditions. With the senators and Roman citizens, and Praetorians as witnesses, I will allow you to end your life by sua manus, by your own hand. I demand you carry out this act at once."

"Accepted," Pilatus answered.

Pilatus knelt. A guard handed him a dagger. He gained self-confidence as he thought, *Procula is certain this will work. I will survive this.* He focused on his ring with two garnets. *There is strength in the red flame. There is life in the green sparkle of the sea, like Procula's green eyes.* Pilatus carefully opened his toga, making sure he did not lean forward and reveal the lining under his tunic. As he thrust the blade into his abdomen, his mind screamed. *Drusilla is not here! Did Caligula suspect her collaboration? Did Chaerea lie about his support?* With sudden fear, Pilatus abandoned his plan of deception, decided to make the suicide real, and pushed the dagger deeper.

Caligula left his curule chair, stood over Pilatus, and peered at him with a malevolent smile of satisfaction. Pilatus groaned as he lay on the floor. The blood stain on his toga and the pooling on the floor contrasted with the pristine white of his immaculate garment. Caligula leaned closer and whispered. "Yes, the Praetorians, the people, and Senate will insist I follow tradition. I will not confiscate your estate and I will not exterminate your family, but I will take care of Procula. After I am through with her, she will not even remember you. Goodbye, Pilatus."

Rage engulfed Pilatus. Groaning with real pain, he slowly rose to one knee. He pulled the bloody dagger out of his body and his balance wavering, pointed it at Caligula. Caligula stepped backwards, looking down at Pilatus and bellowed, "What is this? Tribune, give me your sword, I will finish him myself."

Chaerea drew his short sword. As he approached Caligula, the Tribune held the sword by its blade and offered the handle to the emperor. When Caligula reached for the handle, Chaerea flipped the sword over, caught the handle, and plunged the blade into Caligula's heart. The emperor collapsed onto the floor as a pool of blood formed around him. Chaerea shouted, "The bastard is dead!"

Procula ran to her husband. Nigrinus and Metellanus were close behind. She hugged her husband, soaking her dress with blood. Procula sobbed, "What made you threaten Caligula? Why didn't you follow the plan?"

Concerned her husband did not answer, she peeled back the

liner and discovered his wound. "No! He is really injured! He thrust the dagger in too deep! Help us!"

Together she and Metellanus cut open Pilatus's tunic and found where the dagger had pierced his abdomen. Procula removed her shroud and pressed it against Pilatus's wound. Metellanus and Procula stemmed the flow of blood. Nigrinus said, "Good. The liner prevented deep penetration of the dagger, but we should not move him until he has been examined by a doctor. Metellanus, see if the Praetorians have a physician."

Nigrinus watched as the Praetorian guards led Caligula's uncle to the curule chair. They declared Tiberius Claudius Nero Germanicus as Caligula's chosen successor. Nigrinus said, "A victory for the Pontii. A defeat for the Republic."

Pilatus asked Nigrinus, "What did you mean, cousin, 'A defeat for the Republic'?"

"First we must save your life. I will explain later."

A military doctor, who had been with the Praetorian guards, promptly arrived with his kit. He gave Pilatus a wine skin and urged him to drink heavily before he began. The doctor soaked a sponge with vinegar and pushed it into Pilatus's wound. He removed the sponge, repeated the sanitization procedure two more times with clean sponges. As the doctor sutured the puncture he laughed. "I thought my assignment was going to pronounce you dead, not to save you."

The doctor finished the sutures and examined his work. "Sutures will not be enough. Merely sitting could open the wound." He removed three curved metal clasps from his kit and laughed. You can cash in these clasps when your wound heals. They are silver."

As the doctor clamped his wound, Pilatus was now only halfway through the wine skin and the pain caused him to groan. The surgeon wrapped his abdomen with clean linen. Pilatus asked, "Why silver?"

"There are doctors who have the opinion that using the precious metal honors Asclepius, the god of medicine, who will then promote healing. Humph! Hippocrates wrote, 'Science is the father of knowledge, but opinion breeds ignorance.' In my experience, silver works best, and not because of a myth. You should recover, if you get the bandages changed every other day. I've seen many wounds deeper and the soldiers survived."

"Thank you, Doctor."

"Thank you! We don't have Caligula around anymore."

Pilatus lay on his back and said, "Nigrinus, cousin, now tell me what you meant by your comment on the Republic."

"We exploited your ruse as part of a plan to remove Caligula. We were expecting the leaders of the Senate to proclaim the return of the Republic. But they are nowhere to be seen. So instead of a new republic, the Praetorians are exclaiming Claudius the new emperor."

Pilatus tried to sit up, but grunted and lay down as he said, "What? I was expendable? My life, my family, our clan, all at risk?"

Nigrinus said, "Cousin, yes, we were at risk. But we are rid of Caligula. You'll live. Take another swig of wine."

Procula glared at Nigrinus and said, "Husband, your cousin told Metallanus and me nothing about this plot. All our efforts were only to convince Caligula that you had committed suicide."

Nigrinus said, "Chaerea, and I, and a handful of powerful senators conspired to assassinate Caligula. Independent of our plot, Drusilla devised the sham suicide to save Procula and prevent your execution by Caligula. When Procula told us, we took advantage. Pilatus, your act was so real, it looked like Caligula was interfering and had broken with the tradition of sua manus. It was then easy for Chaerea. He was certain the Praetorians would be against Caligula. Pilatus, you rewrote the script. That was brilliant!"

Pilatus said, "I saw that Drusilla was absent. She is always with him, and she was the key to our plan. So I assumed Caligula had discovered the ploy and had killed her. Then I tried to kill myself. After that I did not have to act."

"Now we will have Claudius as emperor," said Nigrinus. For years he has survived Caligula's purging of family members by feigning as being dull witted. He did not know of our plan, but with Caligula's assassination, Claudius shrugged off his mental malady and assumed the role of emperor. Let us hope he rules in the manner of Augustus and not the last two emperors."

#

Over the next month after Caligula's assassination, Pilatus stayed at home to heal and did not attend the bath for several weeks. He sent for Marianus to live with him in Rome, joining Arena and Livia who still lived at the Pontius house. Pilatus discovered that Drusilla had missed his aborted suicide due to severe illness. She had never recovered and had died.

Pilatus eventually attended the public baths again and returned home energized. He sat with Procula in their garden courtyard. Pilatus said, "After today's gathering at the baths, I can see that the upper echelon of Roman society has been reassured by Caligula's removal. People are more relaxed and confident.

Investment in building projects that are beneficial to Rome, not to a madman's weird fetishes, are underway. Claudius is allowing the Senate and government to return to their normal functions. It is stabilizing Rome."

Procula said, "You were very careful, correct? Are you still mad at Nigrinus? You didn't wrestle your cousin, did you? The doctor said you need several more weeks of healing before you are able to exercise."

Pilatus answered, "No! Of course, n . . . " He stopped, realizing she was teasing.

"Procula, while waiting for my wound to heal, I recalled your talk at the inn on Jesus's teachings. I am interested in the religious sect's concepts. Do they have any documents I can read?"

Procula looked pleased and said, "I do not know of any writings. Why don't you attend one of the meetings with me? They have been held at Priscilla's house for months."

"No. I do not want to be recognized at one of these meetings. Priscilla? What is her family name?"

"Priscilla and her husband Aquila are Jews from Pontus. They are tent makers."

Pilatus commented, "Hah, just a coincidence, but I have read there was a Tribune of the Plebs in Caesar Julius's time, named Aquila, Pontius Aquila. But none of my family has ever mentioned him as a relation, which is not surprising, because he joined the Liberatores in assassinating Caesar."

Procula continued, "We could arrange a private meeting with the couple."

"How are they going to react when they meet the man who

ordered Jesus crucified? They must know my role in his trial. Won't they be offended?"

"They believe in God's plan and we all are part of it. You will see that when you meet them. They live the words preached by Jesus. Love your neighbor as yourself."

Pilatus said, "Let's go tomorrow."

#

Pilatus was familiar with the way to the Quirinal Hill where Priscilla and Aquila lived. He had taken the same route to the Castra Praetoria, passing through the Subura neighborhood, along the lower reaches of the Quirinal Hill and then exiting the northeast city gate to reach the castra. Procula did not want to use litters. She was not timid and preferred to walk. Pilatus had two guards precede them and Metellanus followed.

The entourage departed their affluent neighborhood on the Palatine Hill, crossed the center of the city among the government buildings in the Forum, and entered the narrow, crowded streets of Subura. The delicious aroma of baked bread and the food of street vendors was in the air. When they passed alleys, the aromas were interrupted by an influx of foul odors. Pilatus stopped at a six-pointed star on a building front he had passed many times, but had never paid attention, and asked, "Procula, why aren't the meetings held at this synagogue?"

"Aquila, being a Jew, discussed Jesus's teachings at the synagogue a few times. His message did not please the patrons. Because Jews do not allow Gentiles to enter the synagogue, the Christianos meetings are held in people's homes so that Jews, Romans, free citizens, and slaves can all attend together."

They climbed the Quirinal Hill, a neighborhood made up of

immigrants. Procula stopped at the entrance of a steep side street and pointed. "Their house is the second one on the right."

Pilatus nodded at Metellanus, who posted the two guards at the entrance to the dead-end alley. Metellanus accompanied Procula and Pilatus. He knocked on the door and Aquila greeted them. They entered a large room with benches and tables draped with cloth and leather. Tents, awnings, and wagon covers were in various stages of fabrication. Priscilla introduced herself when they entered the kitchen and living area in the back of the house. She had set a table with food and wine. They raised their cups. Aquila toasted, "L'chaim."

They joined in the toast.

"Yes, L'chaim, To life," Pilatus said.

Aquila smiled. "You know our language. Welcome. I hope you had a pleasant walk to our house!"

Pilatus answered, "Well, uh . . . yes, it was fine."

"Aquila and Priscilla are very excited you are here to visit. In fact, I wanted you to meet them, since they are always happy about life! Every aspect of life," Procula added.

Pilatus directed his comment to Priscilla and Aquila. "I recall that you believe Jesus is the prophet who will lead you to heaven and have everlasting life. It is logical then, if this is true, that you should be joyful."

Priscilla said, "An interesting way of expressing it. I do not know of any believers that apply logic. They just have faith. Also, we believe God is in control of our lives. Whatever happens, we have faith it is his plan. That also makes us joyful."

"In Judea, I knew Christos as Jesus from Nazareth. Christos

means anointed in Greek," said Pilatus.

Priscilla answered, "Yes, Christos is the closest word in Greek that denotes the Aramaic word 'Messiah' or 'Anointed One.' It implies he is our King, but our spiritual king, not a king of this world."

Pilatus recalled the trial of Jesus. "I remember when I asked him if he was King of the Jews, Jesus said, 'You have said so.' But now I understand he was acknowledging he was a spiritual king.

"If it is true that Jesus meant he was the Jews' religious king, not a political king, then not only did I misunderstand, but most of the Jews misunderstood him. They thought their Messiah would come as an earthly king to establish a kingdom free from, well. . . from the Romans or another conqueror."

Aquila said, "It has been said that you placed a sign on Jesus's cross with the words: King of the Jews."

Pilatus frowned, then he said, "Yes, the sign was in three languages. I put up a sign 'Jesus of Nazareth, King of the Jews' in Greek, Latin, and Aramaic – the language Jesus spoke. But now I see why the priests argued with me about the wording. I posted the word melek, for political king in Aramaic, but they had accused him of claiming he was the Anointed One or The Messiah."

Priscilla said, "We understand the confusion in translations. You have heard the Lord's Prayer. Just as we should forgive others, Christos forgives everyone's errors, large and small."

"Madam, you are very devoted to Jesus's teachings."

Priscilla smiled and then demurely bowed her head. Aquila asked, "Did you think Jesus was guilty of sedition?"

Pilatus felt heat rising to his scalp and his teeth grinding. *I have not detected any animosity from Priscilla or Aquila thus far. I think he is sincere with his question. How will anyone know the truth if I don't tell them? I want to tell someone! I have not even talked to Procula about Jesus.* He cleared his throat as his voice caught and said, "No. There was no evidence from his past or at the trial that he was guilty. There were many political pressures from Tiberius. It was complicated. I wanted to release him, but he wanted to die . . . so, so . . ." he pounded his fist on the table. "Why don't you hate me?"

He drained his wine and banged the cup on the table. But he calmed just as quickly and regained his composure, "I am sorry. The situation in Judea got out of my control. I am not going to make excuses. There was not justice that day. I am guilty of abandoning the traditional Roman method of justice: to follow the right way."

Priscilla said, "We do not blame you. You have demonstrated you have a conscience. You said Jesus wanted to sacrifice himself. This was part of God's plan."

"Did you know of the role Judas took in Jesus's arrest?" Aquila added.

Pilatus answered, "Yes, I heard he led the priests and guards to arrest Jesus."

Aquila responded, "He was also part of the plan. Jesus forgave Judas. A devoted follower of Jesus would forgive him also. Jesus would not approve of prejudice, violence, or behavior that conflicts with what Jesus said: 'Do unto others as you would have them do unto you.'"

Pilatus said, "Hmm. I have studied Greek and Roman philosophy and that rule is common, in various positive and negative forms. Sextus the Pythagorean said: 'As you wish them to treat you, so treat them.' Other Greeks, Demosthenes, Diogenes Laertius, also had similar rules in their philosophy. The problem is that people do not follow the rule. I believe the quote from Jesus you mentioned is in the Hebrew Scriptures. I have begun study of a copy of the five books of the Jewish Torah."

"Yes, we have found some common ground! I have older scriptures. You may borrow them if you are interested." Aquila added.

Pilatus smiled and said, "Yes, yes, I am very interested. Thank you, Aquila."

The meeting marked the emergence of a friendship between Pilatus and Aquila. Following several more visits, Pilatus decided the couple's zeal for forgiveness was genuine and was driven by a passion for their beliefs. After several months of private meetings, Pilatus decided he was ready to attend a public assembly.

11 GENTILES AND JEWS

A blaze of magenta streaked with clouds filled the dawn sky above the courtyard. As the morning brightened, Pilatus gazed at the reflections in the peristylium's pool. His thoughts returned to several years earlier, to the day that Caligula had ordered him to commit suicide.

I am free of that fear now. I am living my new life. Procula and I have always been in love, but the last few years we have also bonded together spiritually, with Jesus's teachings. Our lives are richer having adopted Marianus. Livia and her foster daughter Arena live with us. Having the young adults here is like having a son and daughter in the house and has enhanced our relationship.

Pilatus sat with Procula in the courtyard of Deaconess Priscilla's house. He noticed how the morning light cast a glow on Arena's and Marianus's faces. They waited with scores of other people for the meeting to begin. Pilatus thought, *A city girl and country boy, but they would be a suitable match for each other.* As they waited for the assembly to begin, Pilatus said to Procula, "This is the anniversary of my first Christianos meeting."

Procula said, "And I remember you commented then that the followers of Christos were very naïve. In your opinion, if they treated their neighbor with love at all times, the practice would put them in danger in the real world."

"True," said Pilatus, "but I have noticed they use the comradeship in the meetings to gain confidence, and then temper their dealings in society with a dose of reality. Now they have become bolder and have begun to evangelize. They have discussed their views in the Forum and on the streets."

"Husband, you have more in common with these people, who show control, discipline, and a better sense of justice, than most of the Romans now running the empire."

"You are right. I have a closer bond to these honest people than to the senators who change political loyalties as fast as the shift in the winds. These Romans that are here now preserve the best of the dying Roman traditions – a strong family, honor, and discipline."

Waiting for the meeting to start, Pilatus detached himself from the courtyard setting despite the clamor of voices. A theme repeated in his mind. *Why was I spared? I was certain when I returned from Judea that Tiberius would execute me, but he died before I arrived. Then I survived a second time. They assassinated Caligula seconds before I would have met my end. There must be a reason for this.*

Pilatus thought back to an earlier time in Judea. *I can still see his eyes on the day of the trial, which now seems a lifetime away. I had determined they were the eyes of a charismatic man whose ego was bent on ensuring his own martyrdom. This vision replayed many times over in my dreams. But, no. Now I see that his eyes exhibited an extraordinary capacity in pity for me. No, not just me, but . . . compassion with no limit, for all of humanity that no person could possess . . . And Jesus had the capacity to empathize even as he was subjected to extreme physical stress. His gaze weakened my free will. There was something about him I cannot define . . . maybe attending these meetings will reveal what is just beyond my perception.*

When Procula gently placed her hand on his shoulder, Pilatus was freed from his dark thoughts and once again noticed the lively crowd around him. The atmosphere in the packed courtyard reminded him of a festival, conveying joy and optimism. Procula said, "I hope we see an improvement over the last several meetings. The conservative Jewish followers of Christos want the Jewish law followed and have interrupted our usual peaceful meetings. The Gentile Christians only want to discuss the teachings of Christos. I cannot understand why the Jews demand that the Gentiles also observe the Jewish laws."

The Deaconess Priscilla led the worshipers through the Lord's Prayer. After she finished, she added, "We call our Christos by his name of Jesus of Nazareth. He is from that town, but he is 'The Christos,' which in Greek means 'The Anointed One.' Anointed means he is our King. But he is our spiritual king, not a king of this world."

A conservative Jew spoke out. "If you call him Christos, or 'The Anointed One,' then you are implying he is 'The Messiah.' We do not believe he is the Messiah."

Priscilla made no comment. She tried to ignore the controversy and finished the meeting with the communio. Procula and Pilatus along with Marianus, Arena, and Livia exited

Priscilla's house with Metallanus. The arguments that had occurred in the assembly had spilled over and had evolved into shoving matches outside the house. Procula and Pilatus separated themselves from the quarrelsome Jews who had just exited. Their guards joined them. Pilatus was confident they could force their way through. But he was not certain they could shield the others in their family from injury. Instead, he engaged the Jewish protesters with quotes from their own scriptures, pointing out that their behavior contradicted Jewish law. Impressed, they challenged him on several passages, which he answered to their satisfaction. After a few exchanges of scripture, they calmed and let them pass.

Pilatus's strategy had worked that day, but over the next weeks, conditions worsened as fights broke out between conservative Jews and others attending the Christos assemblies. Jews who had no interest in the teachings of Christos disrupted gatherings. Other Jews waited outside Priscilla and Aquila's house and assaulted members as they left the meetings. When Emperor Claudius received reports that the Jews were rioting because of their opposition to the Christos meetings, he acted.

#

Two weeks later, a squad of Praetorian guards arrived at the front door of Pilatus's home. Metallanus was speaking to their officer when Pilatus joined them. Seeing the German soldiers in the uniform of the Praetorian Guard surprised Pilatus, until he remembered that Caligula had recruited them from the frontiers. He recognized none of these men who stood before him, except for the Centurion Laspinus Petronius. The German legionaries standing behind the centurion were massive and much taller than Petronius. Pilatus knew the tough centurion, however, and he was certain Petronius had a firm command of his squad. He addressed Pilatus as he handed him a small scroll, "Prefect Pontius, accept these orders from the Emperor Claudius."

Pilatus opened the papyrus scroll and read the short proclamation. He was stunned. All those who had been involved in the riots after the Christos meetings were to be expelled from Rome. Anger roiled in waves from his stomach to his head. Petronius noticed Pilatus's unease and responded, "You are being given an early notice because you are a Roman citizen. But you cannot reveal this to anyone outside of your family or you will forfeit these special rights. When the Jews are notified next week, they must leave within one day. This will minimize the chance of civil unrest."

Pilatus wanted to question the centurion, but hesitated when he saw Nigrinus rushing up the street. As Nigrinus drew close he spoke, short of breath, "Pilatus, Claudius said he would give me time to tell you about the decree before the Guard delivered it."

"Nigrinus, what is going on?" Pilatus said, sounding exasperated.

The centurion departed with his men and Nigrinus ushered Pilatus into the house to discuss the issue in a more private place. "I'll get to the point. Claudius will not tolerate the disturbances the Jews are making during the Christos meetings. The conflicts are spilling over into the streets and have led to several riots in the Hebrew quarter."

Pilatus blurted out, "The unrest was instigated by a few louts! Most Jews and Romans at the meetings have been conciliatory."

Nigrinus looked at his cousin and smiled as he responded, "Ha! Unbelievable! Pilatus, you are now one of them! I knew you were attending the meetings. The things you do for Procula."

Pilatus did not answer as Nigrinus continued, "Don't get

angry, cousin. I suppose you could enjoy calmer diversions, but how can you tolerate the Hebrews after they were so obstinate during your rule in Judea? They wrote malicious letters to Tiberius about you. And you narrowly escaped with your life after the Samaritans almost convinced Caligula to punish you. If it hadn't been for..."

Pilatus said, "If it hadn't been for... what, cousin Nigrinus?"

"Pilatus, you know how much I like to have you around to tease you, and I am not going to... oh, what does it matter. No one cares now anyway. Our late friend Macro and I removed Tiberius before you returned from Judea. Yet we eliminated one evil only to replace him with another – Caligula. But then we took care of him also. I would do anything for you, cousin. I have no brothers, you have no brothers – you are my closest cousin."

Pilatus did not respond, but was thinking, *So to make things quiet, Claudius is exiling all those who have attended the Jewish meetings.*

Nigrinus looked puzzled and said, "Christians, Jews, what is the difference? Don't they all worship this Christos or Christus, Jesus, or whatever they call him?" Nigrinus continued, not expecting an answer, "You do not have to leave. You are a Roman. I was at the Senate meeting when Claudius decided on the expulsion. He instructed the magistrates to direct all Jews to leave Rome and its environs. Claudius assumed the fervor would die out if the Jews left and the meetings ended in their absence. Because the magistrates knew that Procula was a proselyte of the religion when you were still living in Judea, they added her name to the list for expulsion. You know the Emperor has spies and informers everywhere. I convinced Claudius that it was preposterous and he agreed they should have deleted her name! I suspect Procula's uncle, the co-consul Proculus Gaius, might have had something to do with it, since he did not approve of her association with the Jews. However, included in the exile decree are Roman citizens that are Jews, including your friends Priscilla and Aquila."

"Pilatus, what did I hear your cousin say?" Procula had arrived unnoticed and stood behind them. Pilatus and Nigrinus looked at each other, neither wanting to be the one to break the news to her. When Nigrinus explained the details, Procula's mood changed from curiosity to disbelief to intense grief. Pilatus knew Procula would be heartbroken if she could not commune with her friends at the Christian assemblies, and she would be devastated if separated from Priscilla.

Procula spoke as tears rolled down her face, "I will be miserable without Priscilla, but thankfully I will have you, Pilatus, and that's all that matters."

Nigrinus let out a sigh and said, "Someone is coming to their senses. You have a magnificent house, the baths, the city. Besides, Pilatus, how could you live anywhere else? This is Rome. You are used to leading men, and you welcome challenges."

Pilatus interrupted his cousin, "I am wary of the political instability, let alone the menace from the constant change of alliances in Rome."

Pilatus had only one sibling, a sister, and his greatest regret would be leaving Nigrinus, who had been like a brother. Pilatus answered, "I will miss you, brother Nigrinus."

Nigrinus was visibly disappointed and hesitated, but then embraced his cousin and said, "You must be with Procula. I was always envious how you and Procula were so much in love. I will miss you, brother."

Pilatus turned to his wife, "Procula dear, wherever Priscilla and Aquila go, if you wish, we will follow. My visit to Samnium made me realize that I need fresh air. We do not need many material things. It did not bother us when we left our own home to live in Judea. We had each other then, and now we have gained a wonderful family, Arena and Marianus.

Procula brightened. "Pilatus, it seems you have this figured out. We will bring comfortable clothes and items necessary for travel. I assume your sister will manage our household as she did when we were in Judea. Our former family, the slaves, will be happy to carry on, living in comfort. That is a good feeling. We will start a new life with our new family."

Slaves from Greece had told Priscilla that there were followers of Christos in Corinth. It was the closest city with a Christianos congregation and Priscilla and Aquila were certain they could make a living there. They decided that was their destination, and they invited Procula and Pilatus to join them.

#

The first leg of their journey would be 300 miles overland along the Appian Way to the port of Brundisium. From there, they would sail to Corinth. Pilatus bought three wagons for their trip across Italy. Priscilla and Aquila crafted canvas covers for the wagons. Procula, Marianus, Arena, and Pilatus rode one wagon, and in another rode Aquila and Priscilla. Metallanus drove the third wagon with Livia. Although Pilatus had freed his body guard and friend, he was pleased Metellanus had asked to accompany them. Metellanus confided in him and told him there was another reason besides friendship that compelled him to come along. He told Pilatus he and Livia were in love.

They traveled along the paved road at a leisurely pace, stopping when something of interest appeared. When Pilatus saw a large grove of chestnut trees, he halted the caravan. He,

Marianus, and Metellanus went to gather nuts to make bread.

Arena sat in a meadow alongside the road with Procula and Livia as the men collected chestnuts for roasting. Arena's gaze followed Marianus. Procula said, "He is a handsome young man."

Arena needed little prompting to talk about Marianus. "He is very smart! Not street smart like a tough guy who lives in the alleys of Rome, but he is smart in other ways. He is honest, probably because he grew up in the countryside where he did not have to distrust almost everyone he met. But that can be strength too. Although a little thin, he is handsome and physically tough, having lived outside all the time as a shepherd in the mountains. He is adept, quite the marksman with his sling. I remember him saying he was sixteen, two years younger than me. We may be living as brother and sister, but we are not related. He hasn't seemed interested in me, but I have this feeling he really likes me. He seems shy, but his face becomes fierce and his eyes come alive when he twirls around in circles whipping and weaving his bastonem, fighting off imaginary wolves or bandits. His practice fights are so real I can imagine a swarm of enemies surrounding him."

Livia and Procula laughed. "Arena, you are infatuated!" Livia said. "And you are in love, too! Procula, I hope she is not too direct for you."

Procula smiled, "No, no. I enjoyed Arena's concession."

Arena added, "So, do women, proper women like yourselves, do they talk of men's bodies?"

Procula looked at Livia and laughed, "Well . . . yes, we do that . . . when there are no men nearby."

Arena said, "When Marianus swings his bastonem and spars

with Pilatus, his tunic flies up. He has the most muscular legs and rear!"

Livia and Procula laughed until their tears flowed.

\#

Pilatus was eager to return to his collection of documents especially after Marianus's grandfather had given him clues on the background. Also, the Jewish scrolls were of new interest now that he was learning more of the Jewish-Christos religion. These he brought along, safely stored in waterproof containers. They continued south along Appian Way. Although they stopped overnight at roadside inns for security, they preferred to sleep outside in their tents, which had been made by Aquila. At one of these evening stops most of the party had eaten and retired to their tents to sleep. Pilatus used the light from the campfire to study one of the ancient texts that had been translated from Sumerian into Greek. Marianus, Arena, and Aquila sat listening to Pilatus read aloud. When Pilatus ended a story about a great flood and a Sumerian man named Utnapishtim, he glanced at Marianus and they exchanged knowing looks of surprise. "Son, does this sound familiar to you?"

Marianus stood, leaning on his shepherd's staff. He had abandoned his usual intimacy with the bastonem while in Rome, but now upon leaving the city it was rare to see him without the knobby wooden stick. "Yes, like the Hebrew story you read last night about Noah. In both stories the gods warned a chosen man that a great flood was coming. Also in both stories, the man then saved the last people and all the animals in the world by building a boat to escape the flood."

Pilatus sat in deep thought as he studied the fire. "I wonder, did the authors independently write the same story or did one copy from the other? The names of the men are much different, but that could just be language."

Marianus added, as he glanced first at Pilatus then Metellanus, "It must be the same story by people from a different part of the world. Remember last night after you finished the story about Noah, you reminded us of the great flood in the Roman legend? The gods wanted to rid the world of evil people. Jupiter warned Deucalion and his wife Pyhrra, both of whom he considered to have led a moral life. He directed them to save their children and animals by boarding a boat shaped like a giant box."

Aquila commented, "That story is like a legend told in my homeland of Pontus. The goddess Gaia gave birth to Pontus . . ." Aquila went on to tell the story about the devoted follower of Pontus and finished . . . "The leader's name became Lover of the Sea, because he was the most faithful devotee of Pontus, god of the sea."

Marianus looked at Pilatus and exclaimed, "That is the same story Papa told us!"

Aquila continued, "Of course, these are just entertaining tales. There is no god Pontus. The only god is our Lord whose spirit came to our world in his son Christos. However, I do admit that it is an interesting coincidence that in the Hebrew story of the flood when the flood waters subsided, Noah's ark landed in the same area as that in the legend of Pontus."

Pilatus was quiet. *Inland sea, Pontus, in Greek, the name Pontias in Greek means "lover of the sea," . . . in Latin, Pontius.*

Pilatus then unrolled the two animal skins which were covered with what appeared to be identical drawings and maps. He was certain they had something to do with the clan's origins. "I missed that. Previously, I had only glanced at these maps. I knew of the former kingdom of Pontus, now part of the Roman province of Bithynia. The red and green dotted lines drawn on these skins must trace the voyages and ... Look, this green route passes through the province of Pontus on the south coast of the Black Sea. The elder Marianus said Pontus's ancestors went to Troy, here on the west coast, where Aeneas lived."

Aquila studied the maps. "Sir, these relics are wonderful to see. But I am also curious about your family name. Did you have any ancestors named Aquila?"

Pilatus answered, "I have read about a tribune of the plebeians named Lucius Pontius Aquila. As a supporter of the Republic, he opposed Julius Caesar. The archives state he was killed at the Battle of Mutina almost 100 years ago. My grandfather and father used to tell me stories about our ancestors, but neither mentioned Aquila as a relative. Also, I have heard of some other Pontii in Rome, but never met any of them. Nonetheless, my father is from Caudium, and Pontius Aquila was a Sicilian."

The group of men studied the two identical maps drawn on parchment. A route traced by green dots ran westerly across the Aegean Sea. The route then turned north through the Strait of Messina, paralleled the west coast of Italy, and ended near Rome. Marianus had been following the conversation and pointed to one map which looked different. There was one green mark to the left of the route that touched the east coast of Sicily near Mount Etna.

Pilatus, scrutinizing the map, looked closer, "I am not surprised I missed that. I thought it was nothing but a smear, but I see it is on the second map, not as distinguishable, but faded. It was an intentional mark."

Marianus looked at Pilatus's ring and said, "Look, your ring, it has a red and a green gemstone. The paths on the maps, they are red and green."

Pilatus was astonished he had not made this connection earlier. The green route progressed west across the Roman province of Pontus. It then crossed the Aegean and Ionian seas to Sicily and Italy. He exclaimed, "The green route on the map follows the route of Aeneas, the Trojan who, according to legend, was the ancestor to Romulus and Remus, the founders of Rome!"

Aquila looked closely at Pilatus's ring and he reached inside his tunic. Pilatus laid down a map drawn on parchment. "This is a copy of a map drawn by the historian Strabo about forty years ago. It is not much different from the Greek historian Herodotus's map drawn four hundred years earlier, but it includes Britain and the southern lands discovered since the historian's time. Let's see how they compare with the maps drawn on these skins from my ancestors." Pilatus compared the maps. "Could some of the Aeneid be based on the truth? Legends typically originate from some true event. The green lines on the map and Aeneas's journey both lead to the east coast of Sicily near Mount Etna."

Aquila pulled out a small object from his tunic and opened his palm to show Pilatus. Light sparkled from the green garnet set in a gold ring. "My grandmother gave me this ring in Pontus when she knew I was going to Rome. The green sparkling light always makes me think of the sunlight reflecting off the sea."

Pilatus saw a look of alarm cross Arena's face as she clutched her bulla under her tunic. She departed and joined Procula and Livia asleep in the wagon. Pilatus wondered what had disturbed her but then returned to their discussion.

Pilatus asked, "Aquila, what is your uncle's surname?"

"We did not use a family name. The people in my village all knew each other. When I left Pontus to journey to Rome, I introduced myself as Aquila from Pontus, my homeland. It is curious that the man you mentioned, Pontius Aquila, has a similar name. And my green garnet matches the green stone on your ring."

Pilatus mulled over all of this. *Pontius in Sicily, then Rome. The green lines. None of Pilatus's relatives had claimed that they were related to Pontius Aquila. Tiberius, Caligula, and now Claudius, the reigning emperor in power, were all descendants of Julius Caesar. Aquila was suspected to be one of Caesar's assassins. If Pontius Aquila is my ancestor, I understand why my father never mentioned him. And it should be kept secret from the Julii gens, if it were true.*

Pilatus looked at Aquila. "Maybe you and I are related, from sometime in the remote past. There appears to be a journey traced on my ancestor's map from your homeland to Sicily and beyond to Rome."

"Pilatus, we are brothers in The Way. I could not love you any more if we had the same father."

Pilatus clasped Aquila's forearm, then embraced him. *I am surprised that I was not irritated by Aquila's statement. A year ago, I would have laughed out loud if he had said that to me.*

12 CORINTH

Pilatus's caravan stopped for several days in Samnium, to visit with the Pontii clan. His mother and father had been buried on their homestead outside the village of Caudium, located in the hills above Beneventum. The family gathered to reminisce and to visit the graves of their ancestors. Marianus spent the brief time reuniting with his cousins. Pilatus and Marianus used their bastoni as walking sticks and hiked across rolling green meadows overlooking his parents' home. They trekked under a blue sky, specked with wispy clouds. Marianus said, "Are these the hills where you lived as a young shepherd?"

"Yes. I herded sheep, goats, and cattle. Many of the prosperous Samnites sent their children to Capua, Neapolis, or other Greek cities to be educated by Greek tutors. But my father sent me to Rome to live with my aunt for my tutoring. I was not a shepherd long enough in Samnium to become an expert in herding or wielding the bastonem like you. I see that since you left the city, you have taken up carrying your staff again."

Marianus laughed and began to 'walk the circle' around Pilatus, rotating his staff overhead, "This is a good place to joust!"

After a few minutes of controlled combat with their shepherd staffs, they rested. Marianus said, "Sparring with the bastonem makes me think of Papa."

"That is a good memory, son, and be thankful for it. Papa's spirit lives on for both of us in the art of the bastonem. Climb up this hill with me so I can show you a memory I have of my father."

They continued their hike, following a well-worn path and came to a rock-filled brook that cut through the grassy fields. Its cold waters tumbled down toward the house they had left below. Pilatus stopped on the path at the edge of the creek. He pointed to a series of flat rocks in the stream and said, "Years ago, I was crossing this creek with my father. See that triangular rock in the middle? When we crossed, my father jumped over that rock. He told me he had crossed the creek here thousands of times, but never stepped on that rock. He always jumped over it. From that day on I did the same."

Pilatus showed he was still agile for a middle-aged man. He took two running steps, bounced from one rock to another, jumped over the triangular rock, and continued to the other side of the creek. Marianus imitated the feat. As he landed on the opposite side of the stream, he said, "What a memory! Thank you, Uncle!"

#

Pilatus and his family made somber farewells to his cousins, not knowing if they would see each other again. They headed east over the Apennines to Brundisium, the seaport at the southern terminus of the Appian Way. Here they obtained passage on a ship to Greece. Their destination was the city of Corinth, the largest and wealthiest city of Roman Greece. Priscilla and Aquila were eager to visit Corinth, as they knew the city had a substantial group of Christiani.

In Brundisium, they traded the wagons for several two-wheeled carts, which were just large enough to contain their possessions. The carts were then loaded onto a merchant ship. After several calm and uneventful days sailing across the Adriatic

Sea, they disembarked at Lechaion, a port on the northwest coast of Greece. They purchased donkeys for their carts. The party then began a trek of several miles to Corinth.

They followed the road, enjoying the sunny and brilliant blue sky. Workers had used oxen to pull their ship out of the water onto a wooden sled and teams of oxen were dragging the ship along the rocky surface parallel to the road.

Marianus pointed at the ship. "Look, that's the ship we sailed on!"

"Why don't they use wheels?" Arena remarked.

"Wheels would be too difficult to attach," Marianus answered.

Arena added, "They could roll the ship on logs, but it would be hard to steer. See. They made channels in the rock for the sled to follow. And to make it easier for the oxen to drag, the men are putting oil in the channels."

Marianus remarked, "I did not see that! But, I wonder why they are taking the ship out of the water. Does it need repairs?"

Pilatus stepped off the stone road, and the party stopped for a moment. With his bastonem, he drew a map of Greece in the sand and pointed as he spoke, "Here, only a narrow strip of land, just four miles wide, separates the two seas. We came across this sea, the Adriatic. They will drag the ship to the other side of the land and put it back in the water. The ship will then sail to Athens, over here . . . or here to Asia, instead of taking many more days to sail all the way around this southern part of Greece, which is called the Peloponnesus Peninsula. This narrow strip of land, an isthmus separating the two seas, is called the Isthmus of Corinth.

The group continued and it was not long before Corinth came

into view. The city had been built around the base of the Acrocorinth, the rocky heights of the acropolis where the citadel and temples were located. Although not as populous as Rome, Corinth was a large and bustling city. One hundred years before, the city had been rebuilt by the Romans and had been populated by Italians, Jews, and other freedmen from throughout the empire. Corinth was at the intersection of important trade routes and had grown into an international city. They entered the Forum, known as the Agora in the Greek cities, and stopped at the fountain to inquire about a place to stay in Corinth. There they discovered that a man named Paul was to speak about Jesus at the synagogue.

Pilatus said, "Aquila, you said that Gentiles were not allowed in the synagogue in Rome."

Aquila looked to Priscilla for an answer, but her face was blank. He said, "It must be more permissive here in Corinth, allowing gentiles in the synagogue. Perhaps we will find out at the assembly."

They mingled with the local inhabitants at the Agora fountain. Aquila met several followers of Christos, who invited the travelers to sleep in a courtyard outside their house. The next morning at sunrise they accompanied their new Corinthian friends to the synagogue, joining almost three hundred people attending the meeting. A visitor named Paul was to give the sermon. He had traveled from Tarsus, the capital city of Cilicia, located on the eastern shores of the Mediterranean Sea. Paul was a short man with a hooked nose, full beard and long hair. He stood upon a dais so all could see and hear him. Aquila explained to Pilatus that according to Jewish religion, Paul, as all male Jews, had the privilege to talk at synagogues in any city.

Paul's sermon began with the early history of the chosen tribes of Israel, their redemption from Egypt, and the wanderings in the wilderness. He followed with a description of the kingdom of David and the coming of Jesus as David's seed and Israel's savior. He continued with the proclamation by John the Baptist that Jesus was the Messiah, and Jesus's crucifixion in Jerusalem thus fulfilled scripture. He then proceeded with the resurrection of Jesus as promised in the scriptures, the teachings of Jesus, and forgiveness of the world's sins.

A man asked, "You said that it was written in scripture that Jesus is the Messiah?"

"Many Jews do not believe Jesus is the Messiah. He is the Messiah, but much more. A scripture-honoring Jew should know, it is written in the ancient Jewish text of Isaiah: 'For to us a child is born, to us a Son is given; and the government will be upon his shoulder, and his name will be called Wonderful Counselor, Mighty God, Everlasting Father, and Prince of Peace!'

"So, considering his obedient death, God exalted him and gave him the very name of God so that all creation might bow before him and worship him as Lord!"

A man in the audience said, "When will Jesus return?"

"Jesus said that 'within his disciples' lifetimes, within a generation of His passing, He will return.'"

Paul then led the gathering in reciting the Lord's Prayer and administered communio.

After the meeting, Pilatus was introduced to a respected landlord, and made arrangements to lease a house. He then searched among the crowd outside the synagogue and found his traveling party talking with Paul.

Procula said, "Pilatus, please meet Paul of Tarsus."

Paul embraced Pilatus, and his eyes glowed with joy as he spoke. "You are blessed to have a wonderful family, Pilatus! I can see the Holy Spirit is among them. You, sir, are still seeking. Keep an open mind and you will find The Way."

Procula said, "Paul is a tentmaker like Priscilla and Aquila! What a wonderful coincidence."

"Sir, do you have time for a few questions about Christos?" Pilatus asked.

Paul's smile was so wide that his eyes almost closed, "Of course, I always have time for the Lord!"

Pilatus said, "The topics of the Christos's sermons we attended in Rome were primarily about the life of Jesus and his teachings. Here in Corinth I noticed, the history of the Jewish people was included leading up to Christos as the Messiah. The background is very interesting."

"You are very perceptive!" said Paul. "There is a reason for the emphasis on the Jewish history. Unlike in Rome, here I am talking at a synagogue and there are many Jews in the assembly. They will identify with the Jewish scriptures."

Pilatus asked, "There is another difference I have noticed. During sermons in Rome, Jesus was called the Messiah, a great prophet, and it was said that God's spirit lived within him. It was also said that belief in Jesus would reward the believer with everlasting life. But Jesus was not called a God or The God."

Paul glanced at Priscilla and Aquila and said, "That is also the first question your wife and friends asked me!"

#

Procula could not stop crying. She rolled off the blanket

covering the simple pallet of straw on which they were sleeping, stood, and walked into the dark night outside the house. Although her own house was more comfortable and elegant, that was not the reason for her insomnia. Her stirrings had woken Pilatus, and he followed her outside. The full moon cast a beautiful glow on every object in sight. Neither of them noticed the natural beauty, however, focusing instead on her distress. Pilatus was silent as he stood behind her, encircling her with his arms and holding her close. During the last several weeks since they had arrived in Corinth, troubling dreams like those in Judea had returned to her. They both gazed at the full moon and she spoke. "I almost talked you into freeing Him."

Pilatus knew she was referring to her dream of Jesus before his trial. He refrained from commenting and let her continue. "What if you had let him go? I would have destroyed everyone's chance for salvation!"

Pilatus's mind churned as he thought. *If this conversation had happened several years ago, before I understood what the Christianos believed, I might have either comforted Procula or I might have become irritated. But now I am confident in what I am telling her, even though I am not sure I believe the whole story.* Pilatus said, "Love, what has happened is what was supposed to happen. I almost changed what was to be destined. But now I understand I was meant to condemn Christos. God knew that the political pressures would make me condemn him. And Jesus also wanted me to do it. But now it is important that we stay strong and continue. We have important responsibilities ahead. What are these duties? I do not yet know. But I do not think God would have saved me twice from death if he did not have a mission for me. Tomorrow we will talk to Paul." *Did I say that only to comfort Procula? How much of what I said do I believe myself?*

#

In the morning, they met with Paul and shared fresh baked bread and chunks of goat cheese. They sat outdoors at a table made of rough wooden planks, set in front of their small house. The sun was still low in the morning sky and the air was cool. The street was quiet and void of pedestrian and cart traffic. Paul broke apart a loaf of bread, poured olive oil on the bread, and handed pieces to Procula and Pilatus. He said, "Procula, if you wish to feel remorse for an act that almost happened, that is, almost preventing Christos from sacrificing himself, think about your husband. He lives with what he has done. If you think you have sinned, remember I searched out the followers of The Way and had them executed. Christos died for these sins and all the world's sins. His sacrifice is the greatest. Would it make you feel better to consider that you are part of His Plan for our world? You and your husband's roles have allowed this magnificent new age to enter our world. God has given us free choice, but we are all still part of His Plan."

He pointed down the street at legionaries repairing the road. "Even those soldiers are part of the plan. God has brought forth his good news during a time when Rome has spanned the world with roads built and maintained by thousands of legionaries. And the pagan Roman emperors are a part of the plan. Their dominance in the world has brought unprecedented peace to the empire, allowing followers of The Way to have uninhibited travel across the seas and roads to spread His word."

Paul smiled as they all glanced at a familiar scene. On a nearby bench sat Arena and Marianus holding hands. "But you are not done. You have more to do."

#

Procula schooled Arena and Marianus every morning in reading and writing in both Latin and Greek. When they insisted on free time to explore Corinth, Procula was apprehensive. There were many potentially dangerous and immoral distractions in the city. Pilatus's opinion was that they would steal out anyway. He was confident the pair would be safe with Arena's street awareness and Marianus's skill with his bastonem.

On another clear, dry day, Arena and Marianus hiked up a steep rocky trail to the top of the Acrocorinth, a twin peaked mountain, which dominated the southern landscape of Corinth. There they found the Temple of Aphrodite, where a thousand prostitutes lived, though they plied their trade in the city below. They came upon many other lurid activities during their exploration of the city and noted the goings-on, but went on their way. At the base of the Acrocorinth, in the shade of a large and ancient sycamore tree, they discovered a Greek philosopher tutoring young men. They listened from a distance, pretending to simply enjoy the shade of the giant tree. As they eavesdropped, they overheard the philosopher's suggestion that sexual abstinence could bring one closer to God. They glanced at each other with puzzled looks and moved on to find something meaningful to them.

On one of their daily escapades, they bought bread and olives for lunch and sat on the marble wall enclosing the sacred springs of Elena. The city had a diverse populace and Marianus would make up funny stories about interesting and odd looking people as they passed. Arena laughed so hard that she spit out bread crumbs, which then made Marianus laugh.

The spring water flowed into an enclosure, ornamented with white marble and a statue of Apollo. Marianus cupped his hands and drank. "This is sweet water!"

He read aloud the legend of the spring, engraved at the base of the statue: "It says the waters of this spring are Elena's tears shed in lamentation, when she found out her lover was dead. He committed suicide when he found out she was his sister."

When he finished reading, Marianus noticed that Arena seemed sullen. "Arena? Yes, it's a sad story. But you look so solemn, almost as if you are Elena and I am your brother!"

She started to say something, caught herself, and instead shouted, "Watch out!" Arena pointed behind Marianus and jumped to the side as several rocks crashed into the spring waters. Marianus looked in the direction Arena had pointed as a volley of stones pelted them. One sharp stone cut Arena's arm and another grazed Marianus's head. A group of boys near the corner of a building across the street continued to hurl stones. One of them shouted, "Go home you goat lover, but leave your pretty girl with us."

More rocks whizzed toward them as Marianus raised his bastonem. Loud cracks filled the air as Marianus deflected several stones with his staff. "Arena, get behind me!"

A stone batted by Marianus hit one of the boys in the head and laughs erupted from the gang. They intensified their bombardment. Marianus increased his tempo and improved his accuracy with each volley sent his way. No stones hit Marianus, but he bloodied his opponents.

A shopkeeper and several other men shouted and chased the rabble away. Marianus felt the spot where his head was bleeding, but became frantic when he looked around and did not see Arena. Then he saw her approaching from the shop. Marianus asked, "What happened?

Arena smiled and said, "You were routing them, but I did not think you could go on forever. I went to the butcher shop and told the owner that the boys had hit customers trying to enter his shop."

Marianus held Arena's arm, dipped his hand into the spring water and washed her wound. "You are smart. But I have my sling with me. One of them would be dead if they had hurt you."

Arena hugged him and kissed him on the cheek. "That was unnecessary. We worked together as a team. Besides, if you had done that, we could never have walked these streets again."

After he cleaned the gash on his head, he remembered they were to meet Procula and Pilatus at the synagogue. When they arrived, an unruly crowd had gathered at the front entrance. They rushed toward the uproar and could see Paul, Aquila, and Priscilla surrounded by scores of Jewish men who were pulling them down the steps out of the synagogue. Priscilla and Aquila shielded Paul and were absorbing many blows from the mob. Marianus started toward the crowd and shouted, "Come on!"

Arena grabbed the back of his tunic and slowed his progress. "No, there's nothing we can do against so many people."

Marianus felt a strong hand on his shoulder and turned to see Metellanus with Livia, Procula, and Pilatus standing around him, all witnessing the turmoil. Pilatus handed his bastonem to Arena and said, "Marianus, Arena, protect the women."

Pilatus and Metellanus squeezed through the throng to shield Paul and Priscilla with the help of Aquila. Despite the mayhem, they pushed their way out of the crowd without being injured.

Several squads of legionaries arrived and formed lines across the street, blocking escape. The angry crowd was held back. The centurion leading the legionaries, glanced at the bruises on Aquila's forehead and at Priscilla's disheveled and torn clothes. "Prefect Pontius, I am Titus Justus. Are there any charges?"

Pilatus was surprised that the centurion knew who he was.

"No, Centurion. Thank you. We are all right. The small misunderstanding has been resolved."

"Sir, for your own protection and to maintain the peace, I must escort you and your party along with the leaders of the synagogue, to be questioned by the Proconsul."

#

Pilatus entered the long hall with his companions. The Jewish leaders followed in a second group. At the far end of the marble floor was Junius Annaeus Gallio, the Proconsul of the province. He was seated upon his curule chair, looking over papers with several of his Greek secretaries. His seat of authority on the dais emphasized his position of power. As Pilatus walked toward the proconsul, he remembered that for ten years in Judea he had pronounced judgments in a hall much like this one. He now felt uncomfortable as he assumed a subordinate role. Pilatus was a Roman citizen however, and knew his rights and planned to take the initiative.

Gallio nodded, and both groups came to a halt. Pilatus took a step forward. "Proconsul, I am here to advocate for Paul of Tarsus. He has broken no laws. Although Roman law supports religious tolerance, the Jews are causing a problem by their intolerance. I am asking for the security to worship as we please. Besides, there are many Roman citizens who follow the teachings of Jesus. Another important fact is that the assault was directed at Paul, who is a Roman citizen."

Gallio smiled. "I heard you had your fill of the stiff-necked Jews when you were Prefect of Judea. Would you say you exhibited religious tolerance there?"

Pilatus would never forget his numerous conflicts with the Jewish authorities and priests. "I did my job to keep the peace."

Gallio continued, "Don't be so serious, Pilatus. This is rather ironic and amusing. The Jews protested when you merely showed images of Caesar in public. Did you know that Caligula had planned to have a statue of himself erected in Jerusalem ... as a God? How would the Jews have reacted to that? Fortunately, the prefect was smart enough to talk Caligula out of it."

Pilatus fumed. *A statue praising Caligula . . . as a god . . . in Jerusalem? And Tiberius had problems with my conduct? Unbelievable!*

"Pilatus, you and your entourage are free. Do not return to the synagogue and do not make statements that ridicule the Jewish religion. They have the right to worship without molestation."

Gallio nodded to the Jewish rabbis, who stepped forward. "The citizens you drove out of your synagogue have pressed no charges, so you are free to go. But I am sure you have heard about Emperor Claudius's expulsion of those Jews and Christianos in Rome whose deeds were equivalent to your conduct today. I want no more disturbances."

As the hall emptied, Gallio called to Pilatus, "Pilatus, we have something in common. My younger brother is Seneca. I understand you corresponded with his son when you were in Judea. My nephew spoke highly of you."

Gallio stepped down from the dais, and put his arm around Pilatus's shoulder. "Come countryman, let's share wine and continue this discussion. You should have interesting stories of your time as Prefect of Judea."

Later that day Paul spoke in the Agora. Titus Justus stood by with his legionaries to ensure the peace. Justus was moved by Paul's sermon and invited him to speak at his own house, which was in the same block as the synagogue. A week later, however,

Jews again protested. A poster of the proclamation of Claudius's expulsion of Jews from Rome was mounted on the synagogue door, and the protests stopped. Thereafter, Paul continued holding the Christianos meetings at Justus's house without incident.

#

A few months after the unrest at the synagogue, Procula received a letter from her mother. Procula's parents had moved to their mountain estate in Cisalpine Gaul. After spending years in a comfortable retirement, her father had become sick and died. Procula's mother begged them to come and manage the estate. They discussed this with their friends after one of Paul's sermons. It saddened Procula to leave their fellow worshippers, but with Livia, Metallanus, and the young adults, Procula believed their group was versed enough to spread the teachings of Jesus and lead new believers in The Way.

Procula and Pilatus were preparing to visit Paul to discuss their departure when Paul arrived at their house, seemingly distressed. Paul said, "Last night I heard some rumors of a plot to assassinate Pilatus. It was because he ordered the crucifixion of Christos."

Procula gasped. "A conspiracy?"

Paul continued, "The conspirators are Christianos, but they fail to understand that we are part of God's plan, and they should accept His Plan. They also disregarded Jesus's message of forgiveness. I pray the Holy Spirit will guide them to correct their ways."

"Procula just received word that her father has died and her mother needs our help. With this sad news, we will be leaving Corinth," said Pilatus.

Paul looked sorrowful and he said, "I am very sorry for your father, Procula."

I also had plans to leave Corinth for Ephesus to spread the good news. When I heard about the conspiracy I was going to delay the trip, seek out the conspirators, and counsel them. But since you are leaving Corinth, I will proceed with my trip. Priscilla and Aquila are accompanying me."

Procula held Paul's hand gently in both of hers as she said, "Paul, we will miss you! And Priscilla and Aquila, too! They are such good friends to me. I am happy they will be with you."

Paul added, "I believe this is all happening according to God's plan. Be thankful our Lord is guiding us."

Procula cried, "Oh, Pilatus, we should leave as soon as possible!"

Pilatus put his arm around her shoulders. "Dear, we will be safe. I will ask Proconsul Gallio to post guards at our house for the next several days until we find a ship. Paul, if you discover any details, inform me and I will tell Gallio."

Pilatus had a brief discussion with Metellanus, who then departed for Gallio's headquarters. Livia, Arena, and Marianus joined Paul. Livia said, "Paul, Arena has something to ask you."

Arena approached Paul. "Before our family leaves Corinth, will you join Marianus and me together in marriage?"

Paul replied with a joyous smile. "Wonderful!" Paul paused and looked at Procula and Pilatus, then said, "Marianus, the Roman tradition is that the eldest of your family perform the ritual. You may want to have a family discussion first."

Procula's grief turned joy as she beamed. Pilatus addressed

Paul, "Our family would be honored if you performed the ceremony. And after our recent discussion, we should hold the ritual as soon as possible."

"I would be happy to lead the ceremony and give my blessing," Paul continued. "We believe as followers of Christos, the husband must fulfill his duty to his wife, and likewise also the wife to her husband. It is not merely a pleasure to be enjoyed, but a responsibility as well to be fulfilled. Husbands and wives should mutually submit to each other giving thanks always and for everything in the name of our Lord Jesus Christos to God the Father."

When no one commented, Paul said, "Marianus and Arena, those are your spiritual duties. But you are Roman citizens. Roman civil laws dictate that the husband is the head of the family and legally has life and death control over his wife and children. Do you see a conflict?"

It seemed as if Paul was complicating the issue. His comment sobered the group and everyone was silent.

Procula added, "Although we were not Christianos when Pilatus and I wedded, I believe God ordained our marriage. Our parents, like their parents, arranged marriages based on an alliance of families. We barely knew each other; however, I believe the union was guided by God's will. We are very compatible and will always be deeply in love."

Arena asked Procula, "Did you follow the Roman law like Paul mentioned?"

Procula's voice hardened, in great contrast with the affectionate words she had just said about her husband. She exclaimed for all to hear, "The day we got married I warned Pilatus that if he ever, ever, laid a hand on me, he better not even think about sleeping soundly again, because I'd knock him in the head with a marble vase!"

Procula's comment was so out-of-character that her family, feeling uncomfortable, looked down at the ground. Both Pilatus and Procula stared without expression at each other, appearing to contain their anger. Paul stepped between them raising his hands. Then Pilatus laughed and the whole group rolled with laughter. Paul looked around, confused, and then joined in the joke, relieving the tension of the last few days.

#

Later that afternoon, Pilatus waited with his family for Metellanus to return from Gallio's headquarters. Pilatus looked out the window and said, "Metellanus was successful in getting Gallio's support. There he is now with Centurion Justus and two legionaries."

The two soldiers remained outside as Metellanus and Justus entered the house. Metellanus had his forearm bandaged. Pilatus said, "What happened?"

Justus answered, "Metellanus was assaulted by two men on his way to the proconsul's headquarters. They thought Metellanus was you, Pilatus. One of the men is dead and the other is in custody. Gallio requires Metellanus to appear before him for trial tomorrow at the third hour."

Pilatus breathed out, "What?"

Justus said, "I do not see any problem since Metellanus acted in self-defense and will be acquitted. Gallio recommends you advocate for Metellanus, who will give you the details. I have other duties, Prefect, but my two men will be on guard here all night."

#

Gallio wanted a public trial so there would be a record that the families of the accused men had heard both sides of the incident. He insisted on Roman justice, which was to find the truth and base the judgment on the facts. Gallio acted as judge. Paul said he would be advocate for the surviving assassin. He had forgiven him, but felt the man must still deal with the worldly consequences.

With Gallio seated in his curule chair, Pilatus asked Metellanus to describe the incident. "I was about a block from here when I was approached by two men. The one sitting over there said. 'Are you Pontius Pilatus?'"

"How did you answer?"

"Yes, I am Pilatus."

"Why did say you were me?" Pilatus asked.

"Paul had told us last night that there was a plot to assassinate you. As I still consider myself your bodyguard, this was the correct thing to do."

Pilatus smiled and said, "Then what happened?"

"One of the men yelled, 'You killed Christos, now it's your turn to suffer!' Both men tried to stab me with their daggers. I grabbed the knife hand of one and directed his dagger into the other man's stomach. Then I broke his arm, disarmed him, and brought him to Gallio's headquarters."

Paul called on the surviving assassin for questions. "Did you plan to kill Pilatus?"

The man answered, "Yes, but now that I have spoken to you,

I understand that Jesus would not have wanted me to kill him."

Paul asked, "Do you have anything else to say?"

The accused assassin said, "I wish I had talked to you first, Paul. I now ask Pilatus and Metellanus to forgive me."

Pilatus met Metellanus's eyes. Pilatus said, "Proconsul Gallio, for the court records, Pontius Metellanus, free citizen of Rome, acted in self-defense and does not press any charges on the men who assaulted him."

#

Arena and Marianus stood with Procula, Pilatus, and Paul, before the assembled group at the springs of Elena, to declare their nuptial aspirations for each other. Livia and Metellanus watched along with Gallio, Justus and a squad of legionaries. Several Christianos also were present. By Roman tradition, children ceased wearing their bulla after their marriage, to signify leaving childhood behind. Before the ceremony, Arena had told Procula she wanted to exclude the bulla ritual and postpone it to a later time. Surprised, but without questioning Arena, Procula had agreed.

Paul addressed Arena and Marianus, "Anyone who has seen you together could discern that you are the best of friends and in love as well. Express your love by being subordinate to one another out of reverence for Christos. Marianus, love and respect Arena as yourself, and Arena should do the same for Marianus. And both of you, be imitators of God in generous forgiveness and abide in a Christos-like love. Christos loved us and handed himself over for us as a sacrificial offering to God. He came to serve, not to be served, and to give his life as a ransom for many. Jesus assumed the role of servant, even stooping to wash the feet of his disciples. And Christos directed his disciples to follow his model and to wash one another's feet."

Unrehearsed, and to everyone's surprise, Arena went to the marble enclosure and scooped up spring water in her palms. She knelt before Marianus and washed his feet with the clear water. Marianus did the same for her, finalizing their ceremony.

13 FROM THE SEA TO THE MOUNTAINS

The wind buffeted his clothes and whipped through his hair. Pilatus leaned on the rail, feeling the weight of his problems lessen in the sea air. It was a different sensation having a beard on his face and feeling the hair curl over his ears. After he left Rome, he had abandoned the Roman custom of close cropped hair and being clean-shaven. Metellanus said, "People always commented that we looked like brothers. Since we have been traveling, we look even more alike! I never had the discipline to shave every day like you."

They were on a cargo ship headed across the Adriatic Sea to Ariminum, a port on the east coast of Italy. On the way, Paul's disciples Jason and Sossipatros who were traveling with them, would disembark at the island of Corfu to spread The Good News.

Pilatus said, "Yes, it is a free feeling not to shave or worry about your hair getting cut, but it will be temporary. Procula doesn't like me to wear a beard, because it scratches her. But wherever we end up, I hope there will be baths."

Metellanus chuckled, "Yes, it is important to keep the lady happy, especially for those reasons. For me, I love the taste of onions, but Livia says I'll get no kisses if I eat them. I told her that physicians say onions heal mouth sores, toothaches, and low back pain. But Livia said, 'If you eat an onion and kiss me, you will need it, because I will give you a toothache.'"

They laughed. Pilatus asked, "When Paul said words for the marriage of Arena and Marianus, did you consider asking him to marry Livia and you?"

"Pilatus, you have been a caring patronus and friend. My life was good. I did not think I needed manumission, but after you freed me, I found a new identity. I am a new man. And now I feel more like a brother since you have been so generous to legally bestow me the surname Pontius. Livia and I talked about Paul doing the ritual, but I decided that I am a free man and Livia is a free woman. We respect Paul and Christos, but we can decide how we are going to live together as husband and wife."

"That is a good reason, Metellanus."

They returned to gaze at the undulating surface of the purple-blue sea, as the ship's bow plied the watery plane. The sun was bright and cast a glittering array of changing shapes on the surface. Pilatus became absorbed in the flashes of light. Both enjoyed the other's silent company.

After they ate their midday meal on deck, Pilatus opened his shoulder bag and removed the animal skin from among his precious books. Next to the skin he laid a map of the world drawn by the Roman historian Strabo. As Metellanus watched, Pilatus traced the green lines on the skin which he assumed marked a journey. The route intersected the island of Corfu, a location that both Aeneas and Odysseus had visited before crossing the sea to the coast of Sicily near Mount Etna. As Pilatus studied the map he said, "There was something I read in the Iliad about when Odysseus was in Corfu."

He found the passage from the Iliad and read it to Metellanus. "'Ponteus, a young Phaeacian nobleman, competed in the games arranged to honor Odysseus while he was in Corfu.' This is a new clue. The green lines on the map cross Euxinus Pontus, the Black Sea, to the Kingdom of Pontus, to Troy, Corfu, Sicily, and then to the coast near Rome. Our historical records speak of Ponteus in Corfu, Pontius Aquila in Sicily, and Pontii in Rome. These Roman Pontii were already in Rome when Negrinius's family and I moved to the city."

He continued his inspection of the map. "The red lines on the map start in the Alps in Transalpine Gaul and follow the Apennine Mountains along the spine of Italy to Samnium, where my family originated. The red and green paths appear to intersect near Rome. Did the people of these two journeys meet and know of each other there?"

Procula interrupted, "Pilatus, Marianus and Arena are now ready to discard their bullas for adulthood."

As they watched, Arena and Marianus each removed their bullas from around their necks. Arena looked nervous. Marianus opened the leather pouch, pulled out a tooth and held it up. "This is a tooth from my first boar kill. I stunned the boar with my sling and then as it lay there, I killed it with my javelin. When my grandfather caught up to me, I lied, and I told him I killed it with a javelin throw. I have told the truth for the first time. So now I am free. It is fitting that I rid myself of this secret." He threw the tooth, and it disappeared in the foaming seawater.

Everyone seemed pleased except Arena. She held her bulla

against her chest, tears in her eyes.

Procula addressed the young woman. "Dear, you also may have a secret, but it appears you are having a difficult time liberating it."

Marianus placed his arm around her shoulders. The instant he touched Arena, she tensed and then flinched, and just as quickly, she relaxed. Marianus said softly, "It can't be that bad and besides, you will feel better. Go ahead."

She opened her small pouch. Her tears spattered as she removed a ring from the pouch and placed it on her open palm. "My father gave it to me before he died."

When Pilatus saw the ring, he exhaled. "They met. They knew one another!"

He held his left hand beside Arena's open palm. The rings were identical. Both rings had a red and a green garnet imbedded in a gold metal band. Arena said, "Years ago, when I first saw your ring, I thought it was a coincidence, and I kept mine hidden in my bulla. Then one night when we were camping as we traveled to Corinth, I heard you tell Aquila it was your family ring. My memories of my family have returned to me over time, but that night I remembered my family's name and I had nightmares that Marianus was my brother.

"Aren't you angry at me? Isn't it wrong I have married my cousin? I heard you talk about Caligula and Drusilla, how everyone said their relationship was wrong and unacceptable. I believe our love is right, but an uneasiness keeps surfacing in my mind."

Pilatus exclaimed, "What an odd coincidence! The maps, the rings, the stories, they coincide with the historical connections between the Sabines and the Romans. The . . .." His voice trailed off when he saw the look on Procula's face. He stammered a little, but then continued. "Forgive me, Arena. You grew up without parents and a social education."

Procula glared at Pilatus.

"I mean, Arena, uh . . . maybe you and Marianus are cousins, but from a thousand years ago. Yes, yes. The maps. See, if you are descended from the Pontii who traveled along the green lines of immigration on the map and Marianus is descended from the Pontii who traveled along the red lines – if you are cousins, you are separated by over one thousand years. Don't let that worry you.

"And by Roman civil law, marriage is forbidden between those relatives up to the fourth degree of consanguinity – first cousins. You are probably more like one-hundredth cousins! In addition, we adopted Marianus but not you, and Livia is still legally considered your mother."

Procula at last appeared content with her husband's explanation. Arena's sobs turned to laughter as she hugged Marianus and danced him in circles.

#

After two days of sailing, their ship arrived on the northwest coast of Corfu and entered a small cove sheltered by rocky cliffs. Clustered along the pebble beach were the stone buildings of the village of Paleokastritsa. The captain planned to anchor there for two days.

Pilatus's party came ashore and set up a camp at the edge of the quiet fishing village, the remnant of a once larger and bustling Greek town. On the rocky promontory overhead were the ruins of the ancient acropolis of the Phaeacians, the first Greek colonists of Corfu. The afternoon sun emblazoned the white hulls of the fishing boats, beached along the pebble shore. As a cool breeze graced the cove, the travelers set up their tents and stretched out a canopy next to the beach. Livia, Metellanus, Procula, and Pilatus, along with Paul's two disciples, visited the small village. Arena and Marianus explored on their own and hiked up a well-worn path that led to the old acropolis. Later that afternoon, Jason and Sossipatros remained in the village talking with the local inhabitants and the rest of the party joined Arena and Marianus back in the camp. Pilatus poured wine for everyone and remarked, "This is a special wine for Arena and Marianus. We sampled many in Greece, the black sweet wine of Chios, the soft wines from Rhodes, the bee colored wine of Phrygia, and the retsina in Corinth. I savored them all, but I found a wine more suitable to celebrate your marriage. This is sweet Falernian wine, made from white grapes grown on Mount Falernus and favored by patricians."

They held their terra cotta cups as Pilatus filled each one with the aromatic liquid. Pilatus raised his cup and exclaimed, "Congratulations to Arena and Marianus on their adulthood and their marriage. Salute per cent anni! Health for one hundred years!"

The group responded, "Salute!"

They drank together. Then Marianus held his cup, struck a pose, and recited the Roman poet Catullus, demonstrating the education he had gained from Procula's daily lessons.

> *"Come, boy, you who serve out the old Falernian, fill up stronger cups for me,*
>
> *As the law of Postumia, mistress of the revels, ordains, Postumia more tipsy than the tipsy grape.*

But water, be gone, away with you, water, destruction of wine, and take up abode with scrupulous folk.

This is pure Bacchus."

Smiling, they all raised their cups and acknowledged their approval with another sip of wine. Procula exclaimed, "Marianus, I didn't think you had it in you!"

Jason and Sossipatros arrived suddenly, interrupting their laughter. The two men had hurried from the village and were being pursued by an angry knot of people. They had wasted no time searching out new converts in the village, and they had been actively preaching the gospel. Pilatus and Metellanus stepped forward and faced the intruders who abruptly turned to leave, intimidated by the men's postures alone. Jason said breathlessly, "The people reacted so negatively to our good news. We fear they will harm us if you leave. Pilatus, can you stay until we can gain their trust?"

Pilatus knew that if they stayed and let the ship leave without them, it would be very difficult to find passage on another. They were a day's walk from the main port of Corfu. He shouted after the Greeks, "Wait, men of Paleokastritsa, come back and enjoy some wine with us!" They looked back but did not stop as Pilatus held up his wine skin and added, "You cannot reject an offer from Dionysus himself! We offer you Falernian wine!"

The villagers came back at that offer. Procula, Livia, and Arena had a token cup in friendship and then departed for their tent. Pilatus also retired early and lay awake as he listened to the lively and friendly conversations. He reminisced of times as a youth, when he would listen to his parents, uncles, and aunts tell stories late into the night as they sipped wine. The visitors said goodnight and peacefully returned to their homes. Metellanus and Marianus joined Pilatus in the men's tent and quickly fell asleep.

In the women's tent, Arena was excited to share her experience with the women. She whispered to Procula and Livia, "Today when Marianus said he wanted to explore the old acropolis, I suspected he had something else in mind. We took a side trail and entered a secluded grove of ancient olive trees. The sunlight coming through the branches created a patchwork of dark and light splotches on the ground. I felt like I was in a dream world, so calm and protected. Suddenly we were naked. Being undressed outside in the cool shade made my skin very sensitive. Everything happened so fast. It was very sensual and so urgent! We stayed entwined in our secret copse, warmed by our passion."

#

They departed Corfu and sailed north, skirting the Illyrian coast, and stopped to anchor each day before dark. Four days later, the ship arrived at the seaport of Ariminum, at the eastern terminus of the Aemilian Way. The Roman road ran in a straight line for two hundred miles northwest to Mediolanum and Bollonia, the main cities of the Po Valley.

Procula was insistent that they hurry to her mother's estate near Aosta, north of the Po River. Pilatus hired a large coach, similar to those used by patricians and government officials. The carriage was large enough for the six of them. They were to be accompanied by two drivers and two escorts on horseback. Since gathering the crew together had caused their departure to be delayed by several hours, the men and women decided to spend time at the public baths. The baths, like those in Corinth and Rome, had opportunities for physical exercise, followed by a massage and a social gathering in the baths.

At the men's baths, a young man proposed a wrestling match with Pilatus. Although Pilatus frequently wrestled in Rome, he intended to decline. But when he glanced at Marianus who appeared interested, he impetuously accepted the challenge. Pilatus was expecting a sporting competition as in the baths in Rome. As the match began, he picked his clinches carefully, not surprised that the younger man was faster and stronger. In a short time, Pilatus discovered painfully that the young man had secreted finger thrusts under his ribs and had cleverly landed head butts to look incidental as they unlocked and broke apart.

Pilatus avoided clashes as he realized his opponent intended to injure him. He could not determine a way to end the contest, and considered stopping and conceding. Their match had attracted attention as a crowd gathered. When another furtive blow by the younger man caused blood to flow from Pilatus's nose, Metellanus bristled with anger and stepped forward. He stopped, however, when Pilatus made eye contact with him and signaled: "I'm all right."

Pilatus straightened up from his wrestling crouch, pinched his nose with his left hand to stop the blood and extended his open palm toward his opponent, to indicate "wait." But the young man stepped forward and yanked on Pilatus's wrist, spinning him around. From behind, he slid his hands upward under Pilatus's arms and clasped his hands together behind the older man's head.

Immobilized by the double shoulder lock, Pilatus struggled forward and backward and spun the pair in circles without succeeding to break free. In a fair match, grabbing or using the legs to trip was not allowed in the Greco-Roman system, but it had gone well beyond that. Pilatus reached behind for any grip that would unbalance his opponent, but without success. The younger man kneed the back of Pilatus's legs. Onlookers voiced their disapproval and several men from the crowd as well as Marianus and Metellanus took a step forward to break up the fight.

Before they could intervene, Pilatus sunk down, pushed

backward with his legs, and crashed into the circle of spectators. The pair, still locked together, rebounded off the crowd. At the same time the younger man pushed back, throwing the wrestlers sharply forward. Pilatus took advantage of the momentum, lowered his weight, tucked his head, and rolled forward over his shoulder. His opponent did not loosen his hold and fell forward holding onto Pilatus. The interlocked pair flipped over and the younger man took the full impact of both their bodies. The back of the man's head hit the floor and his clasp loosened. Pilatus finished breaking free with an elbow into the man's face. He stood, rubbing the back of his neck. Without looking at his opponent he left for the hot baths.

After a good hot soak, Pilatus proceeded to the massage gallery and asked for extra work on his neck. *"That man wanted to injure me. It was more than trying to show off. In all my years of social wrestling, I have never seen anyone use the double shoulder lock."*

After his therapy, he exited the baths with Metellanus and Marianus and met the waiting women. Procula said, "Pilatus, we met some Christianos in the baths and by coincidence, tomorrow is Saturn's Day. A woman invited us to her house for the assembly tomorrow morning. The meeting is at sunrise and we can leave when it is over."

Pilatus did not bother to remind her that two hours earlier she had been in a hurry to get to her parents' estate.

#

They spent the night at the inn where they had hired the coaches. In the morning, they joined an assembly of forty or fifty Christians. When they entered, Metellanus pointed out the young man that Pilatus had wrestled the previous day. The man had a black eye. Metellanus whispered to Pilatus, "I will return after I tell our hired men to be on guard outside the house, and to be ready if there is trouble here."

After the service, the worshipers filed into the street. Arena, Livia, and Procula entered the carriage. The aggressive young man strode up to Pilatus with a group of men following behind. To counter the threat, Metellanus had the two mounted guards flank them. The stranger addressed Pilatus, "Pontius Pilatus. We know what you did to our savior."

He paused. One of his comrades shoved the young man in the shoulder. He looked back, like a child who was being disciplined by his parent. "I apologize for my aggression yesterday at the baths. I forgive you, as Jesus has forgiven us."

The men behind him smiled, clapped, and were joined by the assembly. Pilatus placed his hand on the man's shoulder and said, "Thank you, comrade!"

They joined the women in the carriage and as they passed through Ariminum, Procula asked, "Pilatus, that started out frightening. What was that about?"

"Yesterday I wrestled that man at the baths and he tried to injure me. On this occasion, he followed Jesus's philosophy about forgiveness. Metellanus forgave the assassin in Corinth. This is all good, but I think only among dedicated believers in Jesus will such good endings occur. I fear this will not be the last time I encounter a hypocrite, a Christianos bent on revenge."

Their route was west, crossing the River Ariminus. From the bridge, the road ahead vanished on the horizon, among fields of crops. The only discontinuity in the waves of green was an occasional stone house crowned by a red tiled roof. Their conversations slowed, quieted, and gave way to the steady hum of the carriage wheels and hooves clopping on the stone road.

They changed horses twenty miles west of Ariminum at the first way station. They sped on and reached the next way station just before dark. The hostel that served the more genteel travelers was full. Adjacent to the inn was an establishment more likely to be frequented by thieves and prostitutes. Pilatus at first refused to let the women stay at such a place. But the innkeeper showed them several clean rooms, and he agreed to rent all the rooms in the small inn to Pilatus to keep out other customers. Metellanus had the hired men maintain guard in shifts throughout the night and it passed without incident.

They spent the next night in Mediolanum, the city's name due to its location midway across the Po Valley, halfway between the Alps and the Apennines. The city was center of the largest agricultural region in Italy. Turning north from Mediolanum the immensity of the Alps was apparent as the snow-covered peaks loomed on the horizon. Their plan was to arrive at the Proculi estate by the end of the third day, but as evening approached it became too dark to continue.

The coach stopped at the Nine Mile way station, its name derived from its distance east of Augusta Praetoria. The innkeeper who served them their evening meal was elderly and talkative. As they sat down he said, "I hope you had a pleasant ride in your coach today. You said you were headed west, so tomorrow morning after just over an hour's ride you will arrive in Augusta Praetoria. The town grew up around the Roman frontier garrison, constructed over seventy years ago. That was after the Roman Legate Terentius Varro conquered this remote valley for Rome. My father was a legionary in Varro's army and when he retired he married a local Ligurian girl. The Valley of Augusta is called Valle d'Aosta and the town is called Aosta. Aosta is a proper Roman town with a theater, a forum, temples, public baths, and an amphitheater. The wines are very good. I will bring you some right away."

Pilatus asked the innkeeper, "Are you familiar with the Proculi estate? Our directions indicated we should go to Aosta, and then take the northeast road, which is unpaved. Won't that bring us back toward this tavern?"

"Yes sir. But that is because your carriage cannot traverse the trail by the more direct way, which is only for foot or horseback. It's less than two miles. Senator Proculus used to walk here and reminisce of his days in the legions, like many of our patrons. He was a fascinating man, with stories about his travels across the Mediterranean. And he tipped well. Yes, he did!"

Procula said, "Scribonius Proculus was my father. We are going to his estate tomorrow."

"You have my condolences, madam."

"Thank you, sir. Do you know if there are any Christianos assemblies held in Aosta?"

The innkeeper had a puzzled look on his face as he said, "What are the Christianos, madam?"

"Never mind, sir, thank you anyway."

"Maybe there are no Christianos this far north. Good, I can do without having to look over my shoulder all the time." commented Pilatus.

Procula added, "As soon as we are settled, I will spread the Good News in Aosta."

The group stepped outside to catch one more look at the mountains before the sun set. Marianus gazed at the enormous mountains in the distance. "The innkeeper said the largest mountain is Montem Album, which makes sense with its white snow cap."

Marianus then "walked the circle" with his bastonem to practice shadow sparring in the fading light.

Pilatus thought it appropriate. "Son, I see that the mountains have inspired you!"

"Those amazing snowcapped mountains!" Arena called out. "The mountains in Samnium are beautiful, but the Alps are stunning! The mountains look so brilliant, so radiant. It is peculiar, but I feel like I can almost reach out and touch them. They are so spectacular, they don't look real."

#

The Alps dominated the landscape as they traveled the next morning to reach Augusta Praetoria. The road passed through an immense concrete gate, the Arch of Augustus. The massive concrete walls and embattlements surrounding the town had been built generations earlier when the town was on the frontier of Roman territory. The walls were no longer needed as the region was now enjoying a period of peace and prosperity. They left the town and traveled on a well-maintained gravel road, passed between two stone pillars, and entered the Proculi estate. The carriage rolled amidst meadows which gave way to orchards of chestnut and fruit trees. On a south facing hillside were vineyards attended by several groups of workers. They arrived at the end of the road where a sizeable vegetable garden spread in front of a large farm house.

The two-story stone house was built on a raised foundation. Along the front and sides of the house were porches lined with wooden columns. A staircase led up to the front of the porch. Behind the house were barns and outhouses, all constructed with stone walls and red tile roofs, similar to the main house. A large dog ran toward them and greeted them with barks at first, but then stopped a distance away and sat wagging his tail, waiting for someone to exit the coach. Procula's mother, Claudia emerged from the house and moved slowly down the steps, assisted by her lifelong attendant. A robust middle-aged man with blonde hair stood at the bottom of the staircase. Claudia said, "Daughter, I am so relieved you have come. Except for my friend Alfia here, I have been so lonely!" She glanced at the man standing with them and stammered, "I, I mean, our guard was here also."

Pilatus affectionately embraced his mother-in-law. Procula introduced Arena and Livia to her mother and they began a lively conversation. Pilatus, Metellanus, and Marianus introduced themselves to Claudia's guard. "Thank you, sir, for keeping my mother-in-law safe. I am Pilatus. This is my son Marianus and friend Metellanus."

"I am Blustiam. Welcome to our valley."

Pilatus said, "Are you and Alfia the only, uh, employees at the estate?"

"My father, Quiamelius and I live here. He is in the vineyards with his workers, who live nearby in Intimelium, a village up the valley about three miles."

Marianus looked over at the dog and exclaimed, "Blustiam, I have never seen this kind of dog. He looks like he is covered in ropes of wool. What is his breed?"

"He is a Bergamascum. The breed is used for shepherding. The shaggy coat is good for the cold, high elevations and the hair over his eyes shields against the sun's reflection off the snow. This dog is not trained as a shepherd. We only farm on the estate. He is, well not exactly a guard dog, maybe you could call him a signal dog." He laughed. "He will bark when any visitor arrives."

Pilatus felt something brush his leg and saw a gray tabby cat looking up at him. "What? This cat has the same stripes as Arcturus back in Rome! What is the cat's name?"

"Callisto."

#

Later that evening after a simple dinner of chestnut bread, honey and lentils, they sat around the fireplace sipping wine. Claudia said, "It was the last batch my husband made before he died."

Pilatus set down his cup. "This red is from the vines on your land? It is superb!"

"We are at lower elevations in this valley where the reds thrive. I will show you my husband's vines, press, and cellar later. These are ancient vineyards, originally planted by the Salassi, the Celtic tribe that held this valley before the Romans arrived. Quiamelius, as skilled as any Roman viticulturist and vintner, has spent his whole life doing a magnificent job managing the vineyards. I will introduce you to him tomorrow."

After everyone had gone to sleep, Pilatus sat before the fireplace, spread out the maps, and continued his research. The cat insisted on napping right in the center of the maps. Marianus emerged from his bedroom and said, "Father, I could not sleep. Are you studying the maps again? Perhaps I can help. I was there when Papa told us the ancient stories."

Pilatus poured wine for his son, raised his cup and said, "Yes, join me, son. Salute! I was thinking. Aosta is on the route traced by the red lines on this map. See here – the route crosses the Alps and enters the Po Valley. This red route represents the mountain people. The red lines on the map trace a path from the Alps to the Apennine Mountains in central Italy. Centuries ago a tribe called the Sabines lived in the northern Apennines. During the early years of Rome, the Sabines clashed with the Romans. One branch of Sabines merged with the Romans. Could the red garnet have been sacred to the Sabines? The deep red sparkle represents the home hearth fire, which in Rome is sanctified in the eternal fire kept by the Vestal Virgins.

"The other branch of the Sabines migrated south and evolved into the Samnites. So, I would speculate that the reverence for this gem was propagated by the folk from beyond the Alps who were ancestors of the Sabines. That would explain the route traced in red from north of the Alps down to the Samnites' mountain homeland."

Marianus summed up, "I follow that story: a tribe crossed the Alps and settled in the Apennines, then a branch moved to the southern Apennines. Among them could have been Pontii who revered the red garnet. But what about the green garnet?"

Pilatus took a sip of wine, then said, "Green garnets are imported from north of the Black Sea near the end of the green line drawn on the map. That line representing a journey across the sea is green, too, because they revered the green gem. My theory is that the Pontii came across the sea a thousand years ago with the Trojans fleeing destruction of their city. Those escaping the war made stops in Corfu, Sicily, and came ashore in Italy with Aeneas. Their descendants became Etruscans and later Romans. Even after many years and generations of separation from their origins, they met the Pontii of the Sabine tribe who had migrated from north of the Alps. Did the early Samnites and the Etruscan Pontii keep up communications?"

Pilatus and Marianus sat back and were both silent, deep in thought. The cat made herself at home on Pilatus's lap, her purring spreading contentment. Meanwhile, the dog napped at his feet. As

Pilatus enjoyed the Aosta wine and the fire crackled in the hearth, he could not think of a better way to finish the day.

14 AOSTA

It had been ten years since their arrival in the Aosta Valley. Procula corresponded intermittently with Nigrinus in Rome, since she knew Pilatus did not write to his cousin. She sat down now to capture her thoughts to compose a long overdue message to him.

Greetings Nigrinus,

It was a joy to hear in your last letter how well you and your family are doing. We are all healthy here, in the cool mountain climate. I am continuing my sermons on the teachings of Jesus in the town of Aosta and have found many friends among followers of Christos. The entire family, including our three grandchildren, Livia (now ten) and twins Pontia and Little Pontius–Pontianus (nine years), make visits to the town to attend the Christianos assemblies. I should say everyone except Pilatus – he has stopped attending the sermons I give each Saturn's Day. Paul of Tarsus, the Christianos leader we met in Corinth, has designated me as Deaconess of Aosta.

My friend Livia and I enjoy working with Alfia tending the vegetable garden, but I miss my mother terribly! It was such a pleasure working with her in the garden. It has been five years since her passing. It was amazing she could live to see her three great-grandchildren.

Marianus, always a shepherd at heart, bought sheep ten years ago, and he has increased the flock into a large herd. His son Pontianus along with four Bergamascum sheepdogs help him. Pontianus accompanies Marianus to the high pastures in the summers. Now nine years old, he is already skilled in the bastonem and sling.

Metellanus continues to work with the estate foreman to keep the property secure and perform repairs to carts, tools, and the wine press. Livia and I both cherish our grandchildren immensely.

Pilatus spends most of his time tending the vineyards with his Ligurian mentor and friend Quiamelius. The rest of his time is spent in Aosta or at Nine Mile Tavern, reminiscing about the battles and old times with other former Praetorians. The number of retired Praetorians keeps increasing as more legionaries retire and move from Rome.

Give my love to all your family, Claudia Procula

#

Pilatus sat in a comfortable chair on the front porch with a cup of wine, his cat Joachim contentedly purring on his lap. Joachim's mate, Callisto, napped on Quiamelius's lap.

"Quiamelius my friend, can you think of anything as wonderful as this? A heavenly cup of wine, a cat purring on your lap, a cool breeze, and a friend with which to enjoy it?"

"Yes, I agree and I should mention that we are both getting old, if we do not also include a beautiful woman in our vision!"

"Q, you don't look any older than the day I met you ten years ago! You were old then and you look old now!" He laughed. "But I must say, your vigor has not diminished."

"Pilatus, you will keep the vineyards going after I am gone. You are passionate about the wine, learn fast, and are creative. As you advised, we tried the white grapes at the higher elevations and they have thrived. Now we also have good white wine."

"Yes, Q, we are a good team. Remember years ago, when I first arrived, Claudia told me the vineyards were planted by the Salassi. When I mentioned this to you, you disagreed and firmly asserted that the Ligurians planted the vineyards, not the Salassi. I did not ask any more about it then."

Quiamelius said, "The Salassi tribe, a mix of local Ligurians and Celts from Gaul, resisted the Roman conquest so fiercely that the survivors were enslaved or killed. My parents taught me to never admit I was Salassi. Our family survived by maintaining we were Ligurians. The vineyards are ancient and were planted by the Salassi. I can say that now. Those fears are gone. We are all Romans now."

The men were comfortable as they sat in silence. That eventually changed as everyone arrived home at once. Procula and Arena returned from Aosta with Livia and Pontia. Marianus had finished the long trek down from the high meadows with Pontianus.

A pair of shaggy sheep dogs came running from behind the barn and greeted the two dogs returning with the shepherds. Callisto, the grey striped cat, scrambled from Quiamelius's lap and ran out to welcome them home. She touched her nose to each of the dogs' noses and rubbed against the legs of her humans. Marianus had brought the sheep from the high pastures to the lower elevations. The sheep would eat hay during the coldest parts of the winter. Their diet in the summer on the high meadow grasses gave a special flavor to the soft cheese made from their milk, which Pilatus savored. Marianus and Pontianus climbed the stairs to the porch. Pilatus called out and held up his cup. "Salute! I'm glad you're back, boys."

His grandson Pontianus responded, "We missed you, too, Papa."

Pilatus said, "Missed you? Uh . . . no, I was out of the delicious soft cheese."

His grandson said, "You boasted you could eat the legionaries' hard cheese while the sheep were gone. But, I guess those old teeth of yours can only chew the soft cheese."

Pilatus laughed. Marianus threw his bastonem to Pontianus and added, "We ran out of wine weeks ago, please pour me a cup."

Pontianus propped the bastoni against the porch railing. He and Marianus sank down into chairs next to Pilatus. Marianus exhaled, "We walked twenty miles today and we find you here sipping wine."

"Yeah, Papa, what are you doing? Do you think you're retired?" Pontianus added.

Pilatus shot back, "Twenty miles? Sure, twenty miles all downhill! At least I have a gentleman's occupation, you smell like, like, uh . . . let me think, oh yeah, like shepherds."

"You are a gentleman? Is that why you have purple feet?" said Arena as she and Procula walked up the steps to the portico. Arena kissed Marianus and Pontianus wiggled away as she embraced him.

Pilatus poured a tiny bit of wine into a cup of water for Pontianus and a stronger mixture for Marianus. He smiled as he called to Procula, "My love, sit down and join us!"

Their eyes met. Even after thirty-six years of marriage their eye contact still caused a deep stir in Pilatus. Procula gave him a quick kiss and continued into the house as she answered, "I have too much to do right now. I bought fresh bread and olives that I will bring out after the boys take a bath to rid them of the sheep smell."

Pontianus knew his twin sister could hear him when he said, "What about the girls taking a bath? Didn't all that talking in town get them dirty?" He then crouched down as his twin sister stomped up to confront him.

Pontia snapped back, "Hey, you better watch it, brother! You're back for the winter and can't run off to the mountains to get away from me." She picked up his bastonem, and swirled the knobby staff in graceful arcs above her head. She declared, "Besides, I will go with you next spring, so you must put up with me!"

#

Pilatus and Procula had waited for their children and grandchildren to finish their baths and now enjoyed the warm water and companionship alone. Procula said, "Mmm. The water is so comforting and relaxing! I would not be able to live here without our hot baths."

Pilatus said, "I recall that when we first arrived at the estate, it was necessary to take our baths in the afternoon. We waited for the farmhands to finish in the fields, so they could stoke the hypocaust furnace under the house and heat the water.

"But now we can have hot water any time, thanks to Marianus who found that hot spring high in the hills. He visited the Ponte del Ponde, the nearby aqueduct, and talked to the aquarius. Marianus then adapted the engineer's design and built a small system to carry hot water to the house. We owe him our gratitude."

Procula said, "Marianus is smart and resourceful. And remember? After Marianus showed the aquarius his hot water system, the engineer offered him an apprenticeship. But he would rather shepherd and spend more time with his growing son. And Arena, she has shown innate intelligence and adjusts well to changes, which may be due to the hardships she endured in her youth.

"Our grandchildren must have inherited talent from their parents. Do you remember when Arena insisted I teach them all to read and write in Latin and Greek as soon as they could talk both languages? I thought it was too early, since they were three and Livia four, but they all learned quickly."

Pilatus laughed, "It's amusing. When we are alone, away from the children and grandchildren, we still talk about them. We never tire of talking about them. And they are very loving. After we didn't have children, I would have never dreamed of our life as it is now. We are incredibly lucky."

Procula hugged him and said, "Yes, Jesus has blessed us!"

#

They finished their evening meal, the first the family had shared in a month, and sat around the table talking about everything from Christos's teachings to Pontianus boasting he hit a vulture in flight with his sling. The talk turned to sheep raising, milking, and cheese making. They decided that a few aged sheep that were not producing milk would be slaughtered for meat and discussed the spring birthing of the sheep. Marianus looked at Pontianus and said, "Do you remember the first time you saw a lamb born?"

"No."

"When you were about three, you were watching as an ewe gave birth and I helped ease out the lamb. After the lamb came out, you gasped and said, 'How fast was that lamb running when he hit that sheep?'"

Pontia groaned, "Father, you told us that joke before!"

Later that evening Procula and Pilatus sat on the portico enjoying the cool mountain air. Pilatus took in a deep breath and exhaled with a sigh of contentment. She broke the silence, "A Praetorian from Rome attended the meeting today in Aosta."

"So? That is not unusual."

"The man said Paul baptized him in Rome."

Pilatus laughed. "That Paul is an opportunist. When Paul's letter arrived mentioning his house arrest in Rome, I was worried at first. But he turned the tables and used the opportunity to spread the good news to the Praetorians, the men who keep Nero in power. Genius on his part."

Procula continued, "There was something wrong about the Praetorian. Although Metellanus was with us, when we left to come home, I kept looking behind us to see if he was following us. I have a bad feeling about this man."

Pilatus was now paying closer attention, knowing that Procula was very perceptive, and he gave much credence to her premonitions. "Tomorrow I will go to town and talk to him."

The next morning, they entered Aosta through the south entrance, an impressive double gate with three arches flanked by two towers, known as the Porta Praetoria. The weather was comfortable and Procula spoke about the Good News to people passing through the forum. Pilatus sat and watched as Procula spoke. She had not indicated that the strange Praetorian colonist had returned. Five men entered the city gate on horseback, one leading a donkey carrying a pack. Two of the men had armor strapped on their saddlebags. Pilatus could see the handles of short swords, barely visible from under their cloaks. He thought the armed men must be in the military. The short, bandy legged, balding man leading the group looked familiar. Pilatus recognized him and shouted, "Paul, Paul! What are you doing here? I thought Nero had you under house arrest in Rome!"

Paul was cheerful and smiling, just as Pilatus remembered him, and said, "He let me go. One of his favorite servants fell from a window while he was watching my sermon. Although it appeared to be fatal, I revived him. Nero considered it a miracle and granted me a wish. I told him I wanted to visit Spain. He said I could go if I promised to return, and he even financed me."

Paul introduced his companions. "Two of my men are from Galatia. This is Cresenius, the Bishop of Ancyra and his disciple Zacharias. These gentlemen are Praetorian guards, Censius and Carolinus, sent by Nero as escorts and to make sure I return." The two guards smiled.

Pilatus said, "You have quite an influence. First converting your guards, then convincing Caesar to let you go, and even getting him to pay your way! Welcome to Aosta. Paul, your visit will delight Procula. Come, she is across the forum."

They crossed the paved rectangular plaza surrounded by markets and public buildings. Paul listened to Procula give her sermon to several score of onlookers. After she finished, the crowd dissipated. Procula was ecstatic when she saw Paul. She hugged him as tears welled in her eyes and knelt to kiss his hands, but Paul pulled her up and laughed, saying, "I should be kneeling down to you. I was inspired by your sermon. You have great talent in spreading the Good News!"

Procula glanced down demurely, then said, "We have so many questions. You look healthy, but I heard they mistreated you in Rome."

"I ate and slept better than usual, but I was not free to leave. My Praetorian guards were interested in what I had to say and some are now believers in The Way." He nodded back to his guards. "After hearing your talk at the assembly, I see you incorporated ideas from my letters to the Corinthians and Thessalonians that I sent you." He handed her a bound codex. I have brought you a copy of the story of the life of Christos, written by Marcus, a disciple of Peter."

They continued their reunion on the way to the Pontii home a few miles away. Pilatus, walking beside Procula, said, "I knew about Paul's letters and read them, and I am curious as to how Marcus described the trial of Christos."

Procula retorted, "For years, you have not attended any of the meetings in Aosta. Your only devotion has been to the vineyards, working long hours. And you have not been reading or studying for years. I did not think you were interested, but perhaps you can read the copy when we get home."

The family was excited to hear from Paul. He told stories through dinner and into the evening about his journeys. The household quieted as family and visitors went to bed. Pilatus retired to his bedroom with a cup of wine and the document that Marcus John had written about Jesus. He lighted his oil lamp and read the story twice. *Marcus wrote the story in Greek for Gentiles to read and included explanations for the Aramaic words. The trial is summarized in two sentences, without listing what accusations were against Jesus. And there is no mention of when*

I sent Jesus to Herod. But, Marcus was accurate in that Jesus answered only one of my questions: "Are you king of the Jews?" His answer was," So say you."

Wait! How could Marcus write about the trial? He was not there! Paul said that Peter guided Marcus in writing about the life of Jesus, but Peter was not at the trial either! And it makes little sense that the Jewish priests would have told Peter the details.

Pilatus had a sip of wine. *Hmmm, unless one of the Jews favored Jesus. Yes, that must be it. It must have been Joseph from Arimathea, a member of the Sanhedrin Council. He asked that I allow him to perform a proper burial and entomb him. Joseph was there.*

Pilatus read the ending again. *Marcus ended the story with Jesus's tomb empty, but he did not write that anyone saw Jesus after his resurrection. Marcus wrote that they would see him in Galilee. But Paul stated in his letter to the Corinthians that Mary Magdalene and the twelve disciples did see the resurrected body of Christos. I thought there were eleven left alive after the one called Judas committed suicide. But the numbers are not important; what I want to know is did anyone see Jesus after he died, or not? These scriptures are confusing. I will ask Paul about this.*

Over the next few days, the family urged Paul and his disciple Cresenius to talk about Christos. Paul was always optimistic and did not dwell on his hardships in his travels. But one evening as Pilatus talked to Cresenius alone, he asked, "Paul said he ate and slept better when in prison? That is odd."

Cresenius answered, "Paul does not worry about eating and does not take good care of himself. He is driven to spread the Good News. When he was imprisoned in Thessalonica and Jerusalem they flogged him. Paul survived being stoned. He was shipwrecked and he endured being adrift at sea. There was always the danger from bandits. But he continued to work hard despite many sleepless nights as he suffered cold, nakedness, hunger, and thirst."

Pilatus said, "He is unquestionably devoted to The Way. I find it hard to understand how he is so passionate when he did not meet or know Jesus."

Cresenius's eyes were tearing when he said, "Paul heard Jesus tell him to stop persecuting his followers. The event was so incredible it transformed Paul from persecutor of the Christianos to a faithful believer in Christos."

#

The second day of their visit, Pilatus asked Paul to walk with him in his vineyards. He enjoyed showing him his favorite pastime, but his real intent was to find a private place to ask Paul questions about the writings of Christos. Before he began his query, Paul said, "Pilatus, you have chosen a simple way compared to your life in Rome. With this change, whether it was your intent or not, you have provided for Procula's and your family's spiritual development. Hundreds or even thousands of people have heard the Good News through Procula's efforts in Aosta. However, I wonder if your own spiritual progress has stagnated."

Pilatus was not offended. He remembered how perceptive Paul had been the first time he had met him. "I had always planned to study and try to understand Christos's message, but I became distracted with my vineyards and with socializing in the town. Thank you for sending us copies of your letters to the Thessalonians and Corinthians. Also, thank you for bringing us the story of Jesus by Marcus John. Your visit raises Procula's spirit, although her passion for Jesus is already strong. I read

Marcus's story of Jesus. May I ask a few questions?"

"Of course."

"You state in your letter to the Corinthians that Jesus is resurrected, and then his followers and disciples see him. Marcus writes that Jesus is also resurrected, but his story of Christos ends with the tomb empty and he does not verify sightings of Jesus."

Paul answered, "Marcus wrote the story with Peter's guidance. Peter and I discussed this dissimilarity before I left Rome and decided a longer version of Jesus's life should be written including the sightings of Christos after his resurrection. We have sent a letter to Matthew and asked him to elaborate on Marcus's writings."

Pilatus said, "So, Jesus was seen on Earth after he was resurrected?

"Yes."

"The disciples, including Peter, saw him – Peter *told* you he saw him?"

"Yes"

"Did Peter say he saw a ghostly image or was it Jesus's body?"

Paul paused, then said, "It does not matter whether it was a ghostly image or if they could touch him. Peter is confident he saw Jesus. In my experience, when I heard the voice of Jesus on my way to Damascus, I was blinded by a bright light from Heaven, but there was no doubt it was Jesus and he was the Lord! That was enough to give me faith. It's as if I was reborn and became a new creation. The old had passed away. Each person must find their own way to be born again."

Pilatus asked, "Which way do you think I should be . . . reborn?"

"Open your mind. Forget worldly identification. Meditate and pray. Thank Jesus for his sacrifice and believe in him. Become a new person."

#

Procula sent a message to her friends in Aosta that Paul would speak in the forum the next day. Believers spread word about Paul's background and attracted many others curious about this man. At the gathering in Aosta, Paul introduced his disciple Cresenius, who witnessed to the assembly his own conversion and described the conversion of others he had observed in Galatia. There was a crowd of young children sitting on the ground in front of the assembly, so Cresenius directed his speech to them. "Children, you know sheep need lots of guidance, and a shepherd's job is to stay close to the sheep. The shepherd must protect them from wild animals and keep them from wandering off and doing things that would get them hurt or killed."

He pointed to them and said, "You are like the sheep, and you need lots of guidance."

In an area where the husbandry of sheep was common, this analogy was easy for them to grasp. Then Cresenius put his hands out to the side in a dramatic gesture, and with raised eyebrows said to the children, "If you are the sheep, then who is the shepherd?"

A silence of a few seconds followed. Then one child said, "Jesus . . . Jesus is the shepherd."

Cresenius meant to indicate that he was the shepherd, and caught by surprise, said to the child, "Well then, who am I?"

The youth then said, "I guess you must be a sheep dog." The

audience laughed.

Paul thanked Cresenius and said, "We must remember how wise children can be. Laughter and joy! What a good way to start today!"

Paul followed with his sermon and finished with a summary.

"Christos died for our sins, and was buried and raised on the third day. He appeared to Peter, his disciples, and to more than five hundred of the brothers and sisters. Last of all he appeared to me. We must prepare ourselves and pray to Jesus the Lord for forgiveness, for the end will come. And then you will see the Son of Man coming in clouds with great power and glory. Our salvation is nearer than we thought. The night is far spent, the day is at hand: Let us therefore cast off the works of darkness, and let us put on the armor of light and live an everlasting life. This generation shall not pass away, until all these things are accomplished."

After his talk, Paul, his disciples and the Pontii family, gathered and laughed as they reenacted the exchange between the child and Cresenius. A man in the crowd drew near their circle, his expression full of excitement, and addressed Paul.

"Do you remember me, holy one? I am Cassius, a centurion in the Praetorian Cohort. You baptized me in Rome. I must tell you of my plan . . . " Paul put his arm around Cassius's shoulders and guided him across the open forum away from the group, engrossed in their conversations. The man appeared swollen with pride as he accompanied Paul, the sound of his voice trailing off as they crossed the forum.

Procula glanced at her husband and Pilatus understood this was the strange Praetorian that had unnerved her. Paul later returned to the group without Cassius. They wondered what the man was about. He explained, "The man just wanted to thank me for my preaching in Rome. He is a very enthusiastic convert."

As the group returned to the farm, Paul confided with Pilatus and Procula. "Let me speak of the Praetorian that approached us. My intuition guided me to ensure he did not contact you. Although he did not say it in words, I know he is harboring revenge toward you. It is like the experience years ago, in Corinth. He had heard you had moved to the area and wanted me to describe you and to tell him where you lived. I wrote a note to Peter on the status of our journey and told this man it was very important that he deliver this note to Peter in Rome. He was eager to do me a favor. Based on his reverence and deference toward me, I am sure he will do that. Peter will show him the correct way. Without guidance, he could spread his twisted ideas of revenge."

Paul nodded at Metellanus and as they joined Livia and the rest of the group, Paul said, "Metellanus has asked if he can accompany me to Gaul."

Metellanus was somber and put his arm around Livia. He quietly said, "Pilatus, Procula, we love you and your family, but we have decided to travel to Caledonia. I am drawn to see my birthland. The news at Nine Mile Tavern is that Britain is now secure. It has been two years since the legions quelled the revolt of the Britains. I have my papers and can prove I am a Roman citizen, so we should be safe. Also, Paul has asked us to spread the Good News."

Pilatus and Procula embraced their friends as tears flowed.

#

That evening at dinner, Paul described his journey to Spain. He said, "I could have sailed to Spain, but I wanted to meet Procula's assembly and spread the Good News in Gaul.

Tomorrow we will begin our journey to Gaul through the pass at Summa Penninus and onward to Vienne. From there we will travel down the Rhone River to the coast and sail to Tarragona, Spain."

Paul looked at Metellanus, who added, "Livia and I will travel with Paul to Vienne and then turn northward. The route should be easy to the coast as there are paved roads and many cities. It has been ten years since Britain became a Roman province, so I assume there will be good roads to travel north across the island to Caledonia. I am now educated and can write and speak Latin. Perhaps I can help my former people who lived in Glen Lyon. A Romanized Caledonian returning home."

15 THE PASS

It had been barely a week since Livia and Metellanus had departed with Paul and his disciples for Gaul, but Pilatus missed them already. Instead of working in the vineyard, he had been in a gloomy mood, sitting at the house and brooding over his friends' absence. But today Pilatus accompanied Marianus to appraise the sheep in the meadows. Pontia and Pontianus, aided by the dogs, rounded up sheep. Nearby, farmhands were cutting hay for the flock's winter food. Procula, Livia, and Arena picked the season's last vegetables and fruit to preserve for the winter.

"Papa, we will slaughter those two ewes before winter; they are not bearing any longer," Marianus observed.

Pilatus nodded. "Son, pick out a lamb. Procula says we are out of rennet to make the cheese."

Pilatus watched Pontia and Pontianus organizing the sheep. "They enjoy this work, don't they? Who is having the most fun herding, the dogs or the twins?"

Pilatus was seventy years old and still in good health. He walked with his bastonem, L'Olivastro, when he negotiated the slopes in the vineyards, but he had not sparred in years. Today, out in the fresh air of the open fields combined with the enthusiasm of his grandchildren, he was energized. Pilatus began *walking the circle* around Marianus, rotating his bastonem over his head and said, "Defend yourself!"

The two men attacked and parried with their bastoni. Work stopped, the farmhands watched with interest, and the twins shouted as they ran to the pair. "Papa's sparring!"

The two men flowed around each other so smoothly it looked as if prearranged. After several intense exchanges, Pilatus shouted, "Aha! You are no match for me! You need your little shepherds' help. Twins, come help your father!"

They hesitated, but Marianus smiled and nodded at them to join. Pilatus moved in circles to avoid defending against his three opponents simultaneously. He changed his center of rotation, interrupting their attacks and foiling their attempts to surround him. The rest of the family joined them and watched the gyrating dance to the rhythm of wood smacking on wood.

#

Much rejuvenated, Pilatus helped Quiamelius and his workers in harvesting the grapes the next day. When he arrived, Quiamelius was squeezing grapes and examining the juice on his palm. Then he tasted several grapes, moving from trellis to trellis to check for ripeness and variations. He handed Pilatus a few grapes and asked, "Master vintner, is this the day? Are these grapes ready?"

Pilatus answered, "All the grapes we sampled are ready." He looked over the four men from the village, relatives of Quiamelius, and added, "I fear we do not have enough workers to harvest our crop in time."

"My grandnephews and grandnieces, and their sons and

daughters will be here within an hour to help. Let's get to work."

Using their sharp knives, they cut off bunches of grapes and carefully placed them in the baskets to avoid bruising the fruit. Pilatus worked most of the day and was fatigued, but pleased. It was approaching sunset as they headed to the house. Pilatus said, "We are fortunate to have such a bountiful crop. Do you think we can crush this many grapes?"

Quiamelius laughed and led him to the winery. Located inside the stone building was a concrete basin where grapes were crushed by foot. The basin was sloped so that the juice flowed out a trough and into the amphorae below. They entered the door and Quiamelius stood silently beside Pilatus. It took a few seconds for Pilatus's eyes to adjust to the darkness. Suspended horizontally above a rectangular stone basin was a tree trunk, a foot in diameter, stripped of bark, and cut six feet long. Crank handles were attached at the ends. Ropes were coiled around the cylinder of wood and attached to a massive piece of squared timber that lay in the stone basin.

Pilatus said, "What? Is this a press? Yes, I see. When the cranks are turned, the rope will drag the timber up the slope and crush the grapes against the side of the basin wall. How did it get here?"

Quiamelius placed his arm around his friend's shoulder. "Metellanus and Blustiam built it. It is a gift from Metellanus. We found a book written by Porcius Cato, *De Agri Cultura,* in your father-in-law's library, which described how to make the wine press. Now we can press the grapes in time and you don't have to have purple feet anymore!"

#

Two months later, Pilatus was at the Nine Mile Inn talking

with other wine makers about his harvest and new press. As he was paying his bill, the innkeeper said, "With such a big harvest, I expect you will have more wine than usual this year. We can certainly sell it, with so many newly retired soldiers moving to Aosta. Oh, that reminds me. Did that retired Praetorian, uh, yes, he said he was a centurion who served with you in Rome – did he find you?"

"What do you mean? I have had no visitors. What did you tell him? What was his name?"

"I thought I would help out and told him where you lived and that you were always working in your vineyards. He did not tell me his name."

Pilatus let out a ragged breath. "When did you talk to him?"

"Why, it was just earlier today."

Pilatus rushed out of the tavern. He walked as fast as he could, then tried running a few steps. He had not run in years, and he alternated between walking and running. Great anxiety coupled with age frustrated him and hampered his efforts. He stopped, caught his breath and disciplined himself to walk at a steady pace. He reasoned, *You will never make it if you don't take control.* It was difficult to keep his fears from interfering. *That Praetorian, that Christianos Paul sent away may have returned looking for me. If I am not there, what will he do to my family? Marianus and Blustiam are home, but my family could be in grave danger!*

Pilatus remembered that the innkeeper had told the stranger he was frequently in the vineyards, so he used a shortcut through a stand of trees bordering the vineyards. Just before he came out of the woods, he stopped and gasped when he saw a stranger holding Pontia by the hair. He held a knife to her throat. Pontianus was ten paces away holding his sling. The man shouted at

Pontianus, "I heard her call him Quiamelius! Who is he? Tell me the truth or she will die!"

Pontia cried out, "Pontianus, throw!"

"Tell me he is Pilatus!"

Pilatus stepped out of the trees and yelled, "I am Pilatus. If you are a Christianos, you will not harm that innocent girl. Would Jesus want you to harm her? Let her go. You can take me." Pilatus threw down his staff and took a few steps toward them.

The stranger shouted, "Stop! Prove you are Pilatus."

"I was second in command of the Praetorian Cohort in Rome. Then for ten years I was Prefect of Judea."

"Keep talking."

"You talked to Paul in Aosta and he sent you to Rome. You were a Praetorian Centurion. Your name is Cassius."

Cassius let go of Pontia, raised his hands, and looked to the sky. Pontia ran from the man. He cried out, "Jesus! I am sorry. He told me he was Pilatus!" Then he suddenly ran at Pilatus, his dagger brandished above his head. Pilatus picked up his staff. There was a whistling sound and a thud. Blood gushed from the side of Cassius's head as he fell dead to the ground.

The children were both crying as they looked behind Pilatus. He turned around. Hoisted into the tree by a rope, Quiamelius's lifeless body was hanging from a branch, with several puncture wounds in his torso.

#

Blustiam and Pilatus both agreed. Quiamelius would be buried in the vineyard. Although Quiamelius was not a

Christianos, Blustiam did not object when Pilatus erected a cross. He planted several grape vines at its base.

#

Pilatus was determined that he and Procula must leave Aosta. His very presence at the farm could expose everyone to more violence. The decision was reinforced the next morning. Blustiam informed Pilatus his relatives would not return to work until he departed. That same day Procula and Pilatus packed clothes and a few days of food preparing to leave the following morning. Procula would bring the scrolls of Paul's letters and the gospel of Marcus. Pilatus included the animal skin sketched with a map that had been passed down by his ancestors. He would not tell his family where they were going, but would maintain contact. Blustiam gave them three Bardigianus ponies, very stocky, strong, and ideal for travel in the mountains. Two of the sheep dogs would go with them. The next morning, they had a long breakfast with their family.

Livia hugged Pilatus and Procula, with tears in her eyes, "Grandmother, I will think of you when I tend your garden."

Pontia and Pontianus handed Procula a bastonem with a simple figure of a fish carved into the handle. "This will help you in the mountains."

Pontianus, always ready to tease his grandfather, said, "Grandmother, you're still young and don't need a staff to walk, but Papa will need all the help he can get."

Pilatus and Procula laughed, and Pilatus replied, "I will miss your humor, Pontianus."

Procula added, "Grandchildren, keep studying the Greek and Roman philosophers. The wisdom of Plato is complementary with

Jesus's teachings. There are plenty of books in Papa Proculus's library you have not read. And help your mother give the Christianos sermons."

Arena, Marianus, Pilatus, and Procula huddled together and embraced as a foursome. The children joined the knot, and they quietly held each other one last time. Pilatus helped his wife onto her pony and to everyone's surprise, Pilatus vaulted onto his mount. Pilatus said, "Pontianus, so now you are speechless? No comment? Those must be tears of laughter. Yes, I know, the vault was only onto a pony!"

They traveled north on a Roman road built twenty years earlier. It was intended for pedestrian and horse travel, and it was too steep for wheeled traffic. Their aim was to reach the pass, Summa Penninus, before dark, a fifteen-mile journey. Pilatus knew there was a mansio available, but they had a tent as a contingency. Snow a few inches deep covered the road for the last five miles to the pass, not unusual for September. They arrived at the mansio, part of a complex of buildings including an inn, barn, and storehouse. The mansio was located on the shore of a beautiful, azure lake. Beyond the mansio complex, at the highest point of the pass, was a small temple to Jupiter. The mansio was maintained for government officials, but Pilatus knew he could get a room, for the right price. If he needed to show that he was authorized to use the facility, he had brought his signet ring as Prefect of Judea. Pilatus entered the mansio and placed several silver denarii on the counter to tip the innkeeper.

"A room for two with a fireplace. And I will need shelter for my three ponies. I want the dogs to stay in our room with us."

"Of course, sir. I noticed you came from the south. There may only be a few weeks more that the road will stay open before the heavy snows. Your dogs are a beautiful sort, good for these parts.

Are they trained to herd?"

"They can herd, but they are better at guarding. And very intelligent."

"Would you be interested in selling them? I could use guard dogs. There are bandits in the hills, even in the winter."

"No, the dogs are too dear to us to give them up."

#

In the morning, they discovered it had snowed several feet overnight. The innkeeper served them hot porridge. "I would not recommend you continue your travel today. The road is passable, but it will be difficult to make good time. You may not make enough progress to reach the next mansio in Gaul before dark."

That evening it snowed again. The next morning, they took the dogs outside and let them run for exercise. Servants had cleared a path to the nearby barn, so Pilatus and Procula walked down to check on their ponies. Another traveler staying at the mansio was brushing his horse. He introduced himself. "Greetings, travelers! A beautiful day! But not for traveling, wouldn't you say? My name is Caelius Quintus, Aedile of Augusta Taurinorum."

Pilatus answered, "Greetings sir. I am uh, Proculus, er, Marianus, um . . . retired, Praetorian Cohort. My wife, Claudia."

Quintus said, "Where were you headed before the snow trapped us?"

"Gaul."

"I was going back to Taurinorum. Are you from nearby Aosta? I know there are many retired Praetorians living there."

"No, we were just visiting, heading back to, um, Vienne."

"Well, good luck. Good luck to both of us in getting through the snow! Oh, and may I ask you? The innkeeper was a rather forward individual. Did he ask you to work for him?"

"No, but he wanted to buy our dogs."

"That is amusing. When he discovered I was an aedile, in charge of maintaining the public buildings in my town, he asked if I wanted to work here."

#

Over the next few days, the snow cover to the north did not dissipate; however, to the south the weather improved and Quintus departed to continue his journey. Pilatus and Procula talked with the innkeeper after their evening meal.

"It is difficult to keep any employees here during the winter. There are five slaves, owned by the provincial governor, so they don't do that much when he is not here. I employ three freemen and a cook. And even if there are no visitors in the winter, we must work hard or the snow will destroy the buildings. Please don't be offended, but while you are here, can you collect hay from the storehouse to feed your ponies and our stock at the barn? My men are busy removing snow from the roofs. I will reduce your rent."

Pilatus said, "Sir, what is your name, please?"

"Berach."

"Berach, we are not offended and we will pay our full rent. We would be glad to help and would enjoy another excuse to be outside. Besides, at our age . . ." Procula cleared her throat.

"Maybe in *your* old age. I like to work to stay young."

"Yes, in *my* old age, and so my *nineteen* year old wife can stay healthy. We like to garden and work."

Berach laughed. "I saw your dogs were out running with joy in the snow after being confined. When I was a boy, my mother used to send me and my siblings outside to play and shout, 'Go outside and blow the stink off!'"

The dogs starting barking and whimpering at the front door, as if wanting to go outside again. "That's strange. They were out most of the day. Is someone here?" Pilatus opened the door. The dogs rushed out and ran north, disappearing along the snow-covered road. The innkeeper sent armed workers down the road, staying within sight of the mansio, to investigate and secure the complex, but found nothing.

Procula said, "I hope they come back soon. It is getting dark."

Two hours passed, and the dogs had not returned. Pilatus and Procula had gone to bed. There was a knocking on their door as Berach shouted, "Your dogs have returned. There is a man with them."

Pilatus dressed and went to the main room of the mansio. A man was warming at the large fireplace in the main hall, drinking hot soup, the dogs nearby eating. Berach said, "This is Flavius Balbinus, the Magistrate of Aosta."

Balbinus said, "Sir, the innkeeper said the dogs are yours. Thank you, a thousand times. Your dogs saved my life! Our party had been stuck in the snow for days. Then the murdering thieves set upon us."

Pilatus asked, "How many were in your party, magistrate?"

"With me there were four. My poor men, they were very

loyal and buried me in the snow to hide me. The bandits killed my comrades and took our horses."

"When your dogs found me, I did not understand what the dogs wanted. They did not harm me, but were not satisfied until I accompanied them. I could not see where we were going and got stuck often, but they coaxed and dragged me through the snow."

Pilatus said, "Are you certain there were no survivors?"

"Yes, sadly. I had already determined they were dead. Your dogs have keen senses. I know they would not have left anyone if they were alive. But I do want to recover their bodies."

Pilatus said, "Let us all get some sleep so we will have the strength tomorrow to find them."

#

At daybreak Procula insisted that Pilatus stay at the mansio and let the younger men working for Berach go with the dogs. They argued on the way to the front door of the mansio. When Pilatus admitted to himself that his pride was driving him, and realized that he might be an encumbrance, he agreed to stay. He sent their mountain ponies with the rescue team.

Late that afternoon they heard barking. Their dogs were headed toward the mansio, leading the ponies who pulled makeshift sleds. Balbinus had slept most of the day and was now sitting next to the immense fireplace. The men who had recovered the bodies gathered around the fire to warm themselves as the innkeeper brought them bowls of hot soup to drink. Balbinus gave two silver coins to each man.

"Men, you risked your own lives for my loyal comrades. Please accept this small reward."

The men were appreciative and gave their condolences to Balbinus. When they finished their soup and departed, Balbinus noticed Procula. He said, "Are you the Christianos who gives the speeches in Aosta's forum?"

Procula said, "Yes, but my husband and I have departed Aosta to live in Gaul."

Balbinus said, "Forgive me for being so impolite. In my delirium, I have not asked your names."

Pilatus thought of what lie he should tell him to avoid revealing his identity. The magistrate would tell people in Aosta about him and the same violence would follow. Procula spoke first, "Magistrate, we have philosophical differences with other Christianos, which have compelled us to leave Aosta. Please do not tell anyone in Aosta where you saw us or where we are going."

Balbinus said, "Of course! I hear my servants discuss the teachings of Jesus. Your message is admirable. I don't have time for another god, you know, politics, pay reverence to Nero. Rome can encompass a multitude of gods. Did you know the temple at the summit of this pass is dedicated to Jupiter Penninus? They combined Jupiter and the Celtic god of the Penninus Alps to make a new deity!" The magistrate paused. "Oh, I'm sorry. I digressed. Is it that serious? You must hide? I owe you my life and I am prying."

"No, it's not serious, but we do want our whereabouts kept confidential. You may have heard from your servants that Jesus preaches peace. So we are avoiding conflict with those we have disagreements. I am Claudia Procula. My father was Proculus Scribonius."

"Yes, yes, a fine man. You have my condolences."

Pilatus said, "I am Pontius Pilatus. Retired from the Praetorian Guard."

"And I am pleased to meet both of you and wish you best regards in your travels. Is there anything I can do for you?"

Procula paused. Pilatus was certain she was deciding if she could trust the man. *I think she agrees with me, that we can trust him.* Procula continued, "Yes. Our daughter Arena will be giving sermons in Aosta. Will you take a letter to her? It would mean so much if you could forward her letters without her knowing our location. I am desperate to know how our children and grandchildren are doing."

"Of course, Madam."

#

Procula and Pilatus stayed at the mansio and worked for Berach. From November to April there were no travelers. They slept much of the time and became romantically close again. One morning they lay awake in bed. "Pilatus, you have not mentioned the disturbing dreams you used to experience regarding the trial of Jesus. Do those thoughts still bother you?"

"Yes, I think of the trial often, but my awareness of the event is different. I am watching myself in the encounter, rather than seeing the event through my own eyes. And I am more of a bystander. It does not give me the anxiety it used to."

"Hmm. That is good. After having read the gospel of Marcus all winter, I think we both can recite the story. But you still do not believe that Christos is God, do you?"

"I believe in his teachings. The philosophy is a just and noble way to treat people. But is the story accurate that Marcus wrote of Jesus? He was not a disciple, and he wrote from others' memories recorded over twenty years after the death of Jesus. And after my conversations with Paul, I suspect the original message of Jesus is still changing."

"Husband, faith goes beyond things we can prove or touch. Don't you want us to have the everlasting life together? Our actions and works on this world are important, but to go to Heaven we must accept Christos as God, that he died for our sins and ask for forgiveness. His grace is free if we believe."

Pilatus rolled to face Procula and embraced his wife. "So, tell me about Heaven."

"Did Paul describe his experience on the road to Damascus?"

"Yes, but he merely mentioned a bright light."

"Did he say it was a bright light from Heaven?"

"Yes."

"He also told me about the light," Procula said. "When I asked Paul if he could describe heaven in more detail, he said there were no words to describe what he saw and that he was not permitted to do so. He did say when we are resurrected and go to Heaven, we will see God. But instead of being blinded, he said, 'We will also shine like the sun in the kingdom with our Father.' We will look as we do now, but it will be our heavenly bodies. That must be what Paul means that we will shine like the sun. As Paul described in one of his letters to the Corinthians, when we are resurrected we will be in our heavenly, spiritual bodies. He said, 'Our earthly bodies are perishable, but our heavenly bodies will be raised and be imperishable. Our earthly bodies are sown in dishonor, but they will be raised in glory.' Everyone will have chaste love for one another. It will be ecstasy forever!"

"Impressive! But did you say *chaste* love?"

"Yes. As in Marcus's writings: 'Love the Lord your God with all your heart, with all your soul, with all your mind, and with all your strength. This is the first commandment.' We will be with God as one."

Pilatus said, "So right now, today, you love God before me?"

"No, no. Together if we love God first, we still love each other."

Pilatus rolled out of the bed. "I must think about that. These last few decades with you have been heaven for me. I could die today and feel life was worth it. Do you want to join me in feeding the ponies?"

#

Winter turned to spring and Pilatus and Procula remained at the mansio into the summer. Numerous merchants and traders stopped for food and supplies. Procula helped serve food at the inn. She discussed Jesus's beliefs, but not Christos in name, wary of exposing Pilatus to further harrying.

After another busy day, Berach sat with Procula and Pilatus sharing their evening meal. Berach said, "It is interesting how things change. A few months ago, I was serving the food to you. Now Procula helps me serve the customers and they appreciate seeing a kind face after a long day's journey. Now we serve each other for our own meals. And we have very pleasant and stimulating conversations."

Pilatus said, "Yes, friend, we have enjoyed your company and you have given us a good place to pause, to study, and to contemplate."

Procula added, "Berach, how are you coming with *The Odyssey*?"

"Wonderfully. For years, the scrolls I had inherited had collected dust on a shelf. But you taught me to read Greek and now I see across the world!"

"Berach, several months ago, you said you did not feel educated because you could not read Greek. By my observations, you are very learned in managing and organizing. Your calculations are accurate in anticipating needed supplies as well as in balancing the inn's books. You are a master in operating the mansio."

"You are very kind."

In late July a letter was delivered by messenger for Procula. Berach handed her a leather tube and Procula pulled out a scroll. She glanced at the letter and saw there was no signature but she recognized Arena's handwriting. *How does Arena know we are here? Did the magistrate tell her? She was not supposed to know!* She looked at the wax seal she had just broken, but there was no insignia. "Berach, who delivered the letter?"

"I do not know. There is no insignia or name. The messenger said nothing, but when he left he headed south toward Aosta."

Procula and Pilatus went to their room. Procula read the letter out loud:

Mother and Father,

I hope you are well. We wonder where you are but hope you receive this letter. Know that we are all safe and in good health. I am sending this message as soon as possible, because a month ago, there was a huge fire in Rome which destroyed a quarter of the city. Nero has blamed the Christianos for setting the city on fire and is executing all those he arrests. Our family in Rome is safe. With all this destruction, it seems fortunate the death toll was only in the hundreds, but thousands are without homes.

The Christianos fleeing Rome said Nero is making a spectacle out of the executions. A tale has passed from Rome that Peter was crucified upside down, because he said he was not worthy to die like Christos. The horrific killings included Christianos slaughtered in the arena by wild animals.

Procula was sobbing and stopped reading. Pilatus held her and asked, "Do you want me to continue reading?"

She nodded.

So much terror and suffering! Paul returned from Spain as he had promised Nero, and was beheaded. Is this the end of the world? Is this the second coming of Christos? Paul said Christos would return before his generation ends. Please pray that Jesus spares us more terror.

Procula cried out, "Poor Paul!"

Pilatus waited a few moments and said, "I will finish."

I have stopped going to Aosta to hold the gatherings. The believers here will continue to pray in their homes. We have many friends that will help us, so do not worry. Do not return. Your loving family, Arena and Marianus.

Procula lay back on the bed and continued to sob as Pilatus tried to comfort her.

#

They prepared their belongings and told Berach they would be leaving. The following day, Berach said, "I am still interested in your dogs."

Pilatus said, "They are family. How can we give them up?"

"I understand. My best horse is my closest friend."

"Pilatus, I recall you saying you used to cultivate grape vines. The next towns, Octodurum and Sedunum, are both in the Rhone valley, an area where grapes grow well. I wish you the best of luck."

"I am getting too old for farming. We are going on to Vienne, but thank you for the advice. I will write to you. Good luck to you as well, Berach."

#

For the next three years, Pilatus and Procula lived in the old town of Octodurum, thirty miles north of the pass. When they had first arrived, a Roman colony, Claudii Vallensium, had just been completed nearby and people were leaving Octodurum to reside in the new city. With many vacant houses available it was easy to find a place to live, and they had found a small stone house that was suitable. The house had a garden with a few neglected trellises of vines that Pilatus nursed back to health, and made his own wine. Procula had made friends, who joined her in worshipping Jesus secretly in private homes. One fall afternoon, they sat outside enjoying the cool weather.

Procula said, "What a beautiful setting with the valley, the river, and the mountains! Pilatus, I feel we are closer now that you pray with me and with our friends. I am happy we found friends to trust and worship Christos together. When we lived at the pass and when we first arrived here, I felt incomplete, just reading and praying alone. But now as I go through the ritual of comunio, even in our small group, I am fulfilled."

"This may be the twilight of my life, but I have been very content these last few years," Pilatus added.

Procula said, "The way you are going, you will outlive me!"

"I don't even like for you to joke about that!"

Procula continued, "You may have outlived most of your comrades in your generation. I wonder how Metellanus and Livia have fared in Caledonia?"

"Outlive Metellanus? He was as strong as a bull! I am confident wherever they are, their love for each other will sustain them well."

Procula said, "The magistrate is very generous to have forwarded us so many letters. And Berach, he is such a friend. I was relieved when we discovered Nero's persecution of the Christianos did not extend outside of Rome. Marianus and Arena and the children returned to the farm and are prosperous and happy. But I miss them so much!"

Pilatus added, "Poor Nigrinus would have been seventy-four this year if he had lived. I owe him my life twice over. He was so infuriated with Nero for not giving him the men and supplies he needed during the great fire. He joined Piso's conspiracy to assassinate Nero, but it failed. How ironic! Nigrinus saved me from suicide, but he was forced to die by his own hand.

"Speaking of the letters, now we can finally write openly to our family again. In the last letter from Arena, she said the new emperor, Vespianus, has not continued Nero's persecution of the Christianos. We could go to Aosta. It is only a four-day ride. Perhaps next summer we should visit for a few weeks. We will not go into town and no one will know we are there."

16 A HOLE IN THE SKY

The next spring as they approached the farm near Aosta, the dogs ran ahead, full of excitement to be home. Pilatus thought, *My God! I do not even know if they received my letter!* As he anticipated reuniting with his family, Pilatus felt the depression which had plagued him for months finally begin to fade. The gloom returned, however, as he remembered Procula suffering from sickness during the winter. Her persistent cold had gotten worse. At the end, she had said she felt like water was in her chest. They had talked about how wonderful Heaven would be. As Procula took her last breaths, he had promised he would be joining her soon. He cremated her and included vines from her garden. Procula wanted her ashes moved and interred near her family.

They buried Procula's remains at the cross where Quiamelius lay at rest. The family spent time together reminiscing about Procula and turned the gathering into a positive tribute of her life. Over the next few weeks, they immersed Pilatus in their lives and activities. Marianus and Pilatus pressed grapes together and inspected the vines. Livia recited poetry to him. The twins showed him their skills sparring with the bastoni. Pilatus sat with Arena as she gardened and they reminisced about their time in Corinth.

One evening as he sat on the porch, sipping wine and with a cat on his lap, he asked Marianus. "Son, shouldn't you be preparing to take your sheep to the high meadows?"

"Yes, Father, but we can wait. The children want to spend more time with you."

"I have enjoyed the visit, but I am leaving tomorrow."

"Tomorrow? Why? Where will you go?"

"I am not sure. The map is not that detailed. But I will know when I get there."

"You don't mean the old animal parchment? That is just a legend. You are too old to keep traveling across the mountains! Please stay here with your grandchildren."

Pilatus said, "I have had a full life, some sorrows, but sharing life with your mother, you, the family, has given me joys beyond measure! The years with your mother were the most wonderful of my life. Now I have a goal to find the source of the journeys traced on the ancient Pontii map.

"I need to discover the origin of the Pontii ancestors. The map shows the source is in the mountains, north of the Alps, in the Roman province of Raetia."

Marianus added, "Yes, the red line drawn extends from Samnium north to the ancient homeland of the Sabines and continues to Raetia. But, Father, this is not detailed enough for you to find the source. You will just wander around the mountains."

"I am confident I can find it. At the Nine Mile Tavern, I talked with veterans who used to live on the Rhine frontier in August Raurica. They know the region very well. The road through the pass continues to the provincial capital of Aventicum and beyond to the Rhine. But I will leave the road before the river and turn south at the town of Vindonissa to Lunernus."

"So, Father, will you please hire a carriage at Claudii Vallensium, after you go through the pass? Then stay the nights at inns? Promise me you'll do that."

"What about my ponies?"

"You sell them in Claudii Vallensium and buy a horse in Vindonissa. Promise me you will travel by carriage."

"Yes, if it will make you happy, son, I will do that. My friends at the tavern told me that a few miles south down the valley from Lunernus there are lakes at the same spot on our map where the red lines begin. Most of the way will be on good Roman roads, except the last thirty miles from Vindonissa to the lakes."

Pilatus continued, "Remember the legend of Lover of the Sea, when the village floated across the sea? They were lake dwellers, and according to the lines drawn on the map, they originated in Raetia. There are many lakes, mountain lakes, in Raetia. I will find the lake where they started!"

#

Pilatus returned to the pass where he and Procula had spent a winter. He had retained some of Procula's ashes. The shaggy dogs accompanied him and chased each other as he climbed to the Jupiter Penninus Temple at the pass's summit. He sprinkled a pinch of her ashes in the oil fire that burned in the temple and thought, *Am I doing this because I do not believe in the Christianos Heaven? Is it, just in case, if one god is not listening, the other is?*

He surveyed the landscape and imagined he could see the

entire world. Below him were all the rivers, all the mountains, all the fields, cities, and seas, even the great ocean that surrounded the world.

From the top of the summit Pilatus shouted, "What world is this? This is not the world where I have lived for over seventy years. She is gone!"

As he wailed, the two dogs stopped cavorting and stood, listening to their master.

"This world has changed! There is something . . . there is someone . . . missing!" Pilatus stared into the blue sky filled with white billowy clouds. He cried out, "THERE, THERE . . . THERE IS A HOLE IN THE SKY!"

His tirade ended. Pilatus firmly pounded the end of L'Olivastro into the ground and shouted to the dogs, "Let's go."

#

Pilatus hired a carriage for him and his dogs, that covered twenty miles a day. On the sixth day, they arrived in the Roman town of Vindonissa. He decided he would walk instead of buying a horse, and he and his dogs followed the valley south through the village of Lunernus and arrived at a mountain lake. He sensed the lake could be the source. For several days, he camped in a meadow on the shore and sat contemplating the landscape, hoping inspiration would come. Pilatus bought food in Lunernus and inquired about the history of the area. The people were Helvetians, a Gallic tribe conquered by Julius Caesar one hundred years earlier. The inhabitants spoke Latin and their native language, but very few would talk with him. An old fisherman, however, told him of ancient legends. His ancestors had lived on houses built on pilings above the lake. He showed Pilatus the remains of wood pilings that had been preserved by the frigid water.

When Pilatus asked the man how old the pilings might be, he answered, "The people who built them lived many, many generations before Caesar."

Some of the Helvetians thought Pilatus was trying to draw the ghosts of these ancient people from beneath the cold waters of the lake, and they were afraid of him.

Pilatus prayed. He contemplated what Paul had told him. *Rid yourself of worldly identity.* His ego was encumbered by his identities. *I am a Roman citizen.* It was a powerful statement that citizens of the Roman state were proud to declare. After days of meditation, he simplified his identity. *I am Pontius Pilatus.* Each morning, he sat before his campfire on the pebble beach and prayed. He also meditated on the landscape of the lake and mountains. Day after day passed. His mantra became: *I am Pilatus.* He dissolved his ego even more. *I am a man.* He accepted Christos's infinite life after death. *I will join Procula in the light.*

On a cold autumn day, Pilatus awoke, exited his tent and gazed across the lake toward the mountains. A layer of fog on the surface blocked the view of the base of the mountains, making the snowcapped peaks appear to float atop the mist. Now he believed what his wife had said: that she would be with her God, Paul's God, and Christos in Heaven. He knew what he must do. He put down his bastonem and walked toward the floating mountains. He entered the water oblivious of the cold, immersed himself up to his neck and sunk beneath the surface. *I will be with Procula in an instant.*

When he opened his eyes, the light was so intense he instantly closed them. He could not feel his arms or legs, nor any part of his body. *I have no mortal body! This is what Paul saw! This is what Procula said Heaven would be like! I am in Heaven!*

He opened his eyes again and something slippery and wet

slathered across his face. He lay on his side and squinted into the bright light, realizing he was on the rocky beach in front of his tent. The rising sun was bright and warm upon his face. His shaggy dogs sat facing him, their long hair wet and matted. He collected his thoughts, *Was it a dream? Now I remember! I thought that? No, it was real. I tried to drown myself!* He looked at the dogs as they both sat and watched him. Pilatus laughed as he looked at them and said, "I can't see your eyes through those shaggy strands, but I imagine the way you stare at me, you must think I am mad."

A week later, Pilatus walked into the lake a second time and woke up on the beach again dripping and cold. His dogs had played their game of retrieve once more. Over the next few weeks, Pilatus repeated his attempt several more times to join Procula. His faithful dogs, however, fished him out of the lake every time. Pilatus noted they seemed to enjoy the game.

The old fisherman, his only friend here, came by one day as Pilatus sat before a driftwood campfire. Pilatus stared through the flames across the lake. The visitor said, "I have some tasty fish for you. I know you eat only bread from the village." He cleaned them and threw the scraps to the dogs. He squatted next to the fire and said, "My people are fire gazers as well. And I see you wear the red stone that captures the Eternal Fire of the Imagination of Man . . . it's on your ring."

This statement pricked Pilatus's mind. Distant memories surfaced as he remembered the reverence for this gem. He pulled out the old parchment map and explained it to his friend, who listened, although the man had never seen a map before. Pilatus said, "Many years ago, there was a clan who lived in a village built on pilings elevated above this lake. Something happened, invaders, weather, drought, I do not know, but they decided they had to leave. A part of the clan went south across the mountains.

They held sacred the red garnet and took it with them to keep their fire, their imagination, alive. The clan lived as lake dwellers in the mountains of northern Italy and after several generations they continued to move south along the mountains, eventually becoming the tribe called the Sabines.

"The other part of the clan left this lake long ago and traveled east down this river, the Danube River. They also had a special reverence for the red garnet. Where the river flows into the Black Sea, they built a village upon pilings above the water, as they had done here. There they adopted the green garnet, which holds the mystery of the sea. Years later, the Black Sea dwellers crossed the sea, journeyed to Troy and then to Italy with Aeneas. Among them were two brothers, each with a green garnet. One of these brothers stayed in Sicily and one continued to the hills where Rome would be founded. Rome and the Sabine nation later joined as one people. That is when . . .

"Listen . . . what is that sound I am hearing?"

"It is a faraway boat, a dugout, bumping against a wooden post on a dock."

Pilatus said, "Say it. Say the sound."

"It sounds like... Pnnt, Ponnnt. Something like that."

"That is when the Pontii, after over a thousand years of separation, met each other. To commemorate the meeting, they crafted two identical rings. Each ring had a red and a green garnet."

The fisherman held out a red garnet which hung on a tether around his neck, and said, "I see many of the red fire stones, but I have never seen a green one as on your ring. Its sparkle reminds me of the emerald lake waters."

Pilatus said, "You and me. We are cousins. Now let's eat."

They cooked the fish and ate in silence. The dogs sat a respectful distance away. The fisherman said, "You have trained your dogs well. They are not begging. And they must be good companions."

"Yes. They know me better than I know myself and they have more sense than I do." As Pilatus said this, he abandoned his plan to tie up his dogs the next morning. "Come back to visit tomorrow and we will explore the lakeshore together."

Afterword: Did Pontius Pilate Exist?

There is archeological proof that Pontius Pilate was the governor of Judea, as written in the Bible, and as recorded by historians Tacitus and Josephus. In 1961, Italian archeologist Dr. Antonio Frova discovered a large stone in Caesarea Maritima (near present day Tel Aviv), inscribed with Pilate's name in Latin. The inscription also extolled he was Prefect (governor) and had dedicated a building to Tiberius. The stone has been confirmed authentic by archeologists and historians. There also have been Roman coins found in Judea, that were minted during Pontius's governorship.

Early Christians viewed Pilate as an instrument in salvation. The Greek Orthodox and Coptic faiths believe that Pilate and his wife became Christians and dedicated them both as saints. Pontius Pilate was depicted in 4th century Christian art next to the biblical Abraham. They were portrayed as parallel figures overseeing sacrifices. There is no authentic history of what happened to Pontius Pilate after he returned from Judea, but there are many legends.

Tertullian, a Christian writer from Carthage, wrote in 200 A.D. in his *Apologeticum*, that Pilate believed in Jesus's divinity. The 4th century Christian author Eusebius wrote that Pilate regretted executing Jesus and committed suicide.

A legend states that Emperor Caligula ordered Pontius Pilate to death, by either execution or suicide, after his return from Judea. Another tradition holds that Pontius Pilate was exiled to Vienne, France, on the Rhone River, where he allegedly drowned and was buried. Other legends assert that Pontius Pilate committed suicide and was buried in Lake Lucerne. The mountain overlooking the lake is named Mount Pilatus. Folklore says he was a regular customer at the Nine Mile Inn, near Aosta, Italy, a town in the Alps near the Bernard Pass.

There are unlikely stories that Pontius Pilate was born in

Spain, Britain, or Germany. The most dubious tale claims Pilate was born in Scotland, where his father, a Roman delegate to Caledonia (Scotland), fathered a son with a Caledonian woman. The son returned with his father to Rome and was raised as Pontius Pilate. Historical research of surnames indicates that it is most likely that Pilate was born in either Samnium or Rome.

Three of the legends about Pilate have him ending up in Gaul, the area now occupied by northern Italy, France, and Switzerland. One location is at Vienne, France. Another is at Aosta, Italy, in an Alpine valley near the Bernard Pass to France. The third location is at Lake Lucerne in Switzerland. Based on all these sources on Pontius Pilate, most probably he departed Rome to live in northwest Italy or France (then Gaul).

There is evidence today that his descendants may still live in these areas. The Latin surname Pontius evolved into the Italian surname Ponzio. There are demographical maps of Italy today that show the distribution of Ponzios is the most numerous near Turin (Northwest Italy in the mountains near Aosta). The second highest density is far south in Sicily.

But where did the surname Pontius originate, or what is the oldest available historical literature that mentions Pontius? In 390 BC, Pontius Cominius is mentioned as a scout for the Roman army during the siege of Rome by the Gauls. In 323 B.C., Pontius Gaius, a general of the Samnites (southern Italy), was famous for defeating a Roman army at the Caudine Forks. Historians state Pontius was a common surname among the Samnites. In 37 A.D., there was a Roman consul with the Pontius name. The most recognized of the Pontii (plural in Latin for Pontius) is Pontius Pilate. The Roman Catholic Church records that a Christian named Pontius fled persecution in Rome to the area of Nice, France, in 250 A.D. He was later canonized as St. Pontius of Cimiez.

There is more demographical evidence that the Pontii were concentrated in northwest Italy in ancient times, as the Ponzios are now. In the history of the Middle Ages, one will find many Pons (the French for Pontius) in southern France, just across the border from present day Italy. The Pontii migrated to southern France and the name evolved into Pons. During the Middle Ages, they were still writing in Latin and the Pons living in France were writing their name down as Pontius. Copies of these ancient documents still exist. One example is Raymond Pons, the Count of Toulouse in 925 A.D. His name was written as Raimundus Pontius. As descendants named Pons moved into Catalonia and other parts of Spain, some retained the name Pons and others evolved into Ponç or Ponce.

These historical characters are a rich source for the stories found in the novels of Lover of the Sea, which follow *Pontius Pilatus: Dark Passage to Heaven.*

MICHAEL A. PONZIO

ABOUT THE AUTHOR

Since childhood, Mike Ponzio has read books about ancient Rome. He traded books and stories with his father, Joe Ponzio, and they discussed the origins of the family surname. Mike traveled around the Mediterranean to Europe, Asia and Africa, visiting many of the locations he would later write about. He continues to travel and writes stories about historical figures, who may have been ancient ancestors.

Mike met his wife, Anne Davis Ponzio, in 1975 at a University of Florida karate class. Since that time both have taught Cuong Nhu Oriental Martial Arts. With John Burns, they wrote and published six instructional books on martial arts weapons. Mike retired in 2015, after working as an environmental engineer for thirty-seven years. Anne and Mike have raised four sons. They are all engineer graduates, following in the footsteps of their Davis and Ponzio grandfathers.

The novels listed below makeup the *Lover of the Sea* series. The title characters are historical.

- *Pontius Aquila: Eagle of the Republic*
- *Pontius Pilatus: Dark Passage to Heaven*
- *St. Pontianus: Bishop of Rome*

For more information go to the author's website:
History & Historical Fiction: Pontius, Ponzio, Pons, and Ponce
https://mikemarianoponzio.wixsite.com/pontius-ponzio-pons
or the author's Facebook page
https://www.facebook.com/historynovels/?ref=bookmarks

Pontius Pilatus: Dark Passage to Heaven

Bibliography

1. Ancient Coins for Education. (n.d.). Retrieved March 03, 2016, from http://ancientcoinsforeducation.org

2. Asimov, I. (1981). *Asimov's guide to the Bible: two volumes in one*. New York, NY: Wings Books.

3. AskHistorians • /r/AskHistorians. (n.d.). Retrieved February, 2015, from www.reddit.com/r/AskHistorians

4. B. (n.d.). Bible History Online Maps, Articles, Images, and Resources. Retrieved February 03, 2017, from http://www.bible-history.com

5. BibleGateway. (n.d.). Retrieved February 03, 2017, from www.biblegateway.com/passage/?search=Mark%2B1&version=NIV

6. Bongianni, M. (1988). *Simon & Schuster's guide to horses & ponies of the world*. New York: Simon & Schuster.

7. Caesar, J., Wiseman, A., & Wiseman, T. P. (1980). *The Battle for Gaul*. Boston: D.R. Godine.

8. Christadelphia Home Page. (n.d.). Retrieved May 03, 2016, from http://www.christadelphia.org

9. Constance Brittain Bouchard (24 November 2010). *Those of My Blood: Creating Noble Families in Medieval Francia*. University of Pennsylvania Press. p. 40. ISBN 0-8122-0140-X.

10. Crozier, W. P. (2002). *Letters of Pontius Pilate, written during his governorship of Judea to his friend Seneca in Rome*. Amsterdam: Fredonia Books.

11. Did Josephus Refer to Jesus? (n.d.). Retrieved May 03, 2016, from http://bede.org.uk/Josephus.htm

12. Enduring Word Bible Commentary. (n.d.). Retrieved February 03, 2016, from enduringword.com/commentary

13. Gensler, H. J. (2013). *Ethics and the golden rule.* New York: Routledge.

14. Grant, M. (1992). *Readings in the classical historians.* New York: Scribner's.

15. H. (2014, November 02). 82 BCE: The defeated populares of the Battle of the Colline Gate. Retrieved March 03, 2014, from executedtoday.com/2014/11/02/82-bce-the-defeated-populares-of-the-battle-of-the-colline-gate

16. Harlan Walker, *Fish: Food from the Waters, Proceedings of the Oxford Symposium on Food and Cookery*, 106 (1998).

17. Herzog, William, R., *Prophet and Teacher: An Introduction to the Historical Jesus* (Jul 4, 2005) ISBN 0664225284 pages 1-6

18. Hippocrates Quotes. (n.d.). Retrieved June 03, 2016, from brainyquote.com/quotes/authors/h/hippocrates

19. H. Johnson *Vintage: The Story of Wine* pg 68–74 Simon and Schuster 1989 ISBN 0-671-68702-6

20. How did the first Christians worship? (2015, December 01). Retrieved February 03, 2017, from http://matthewwarner.me/how-did-the-first-christians-worship

21. I Corinthians: Introduction and Outline. (n.d.). Retrieved February 03, 2016, from bible.org/article/i-corinthians-introduction-and-outline

22. Info@undiscoveredscotland.co.uk, U. S. (n.d.). Undiscovered Scotland. Retrieved April, 2015, from http://www.undiscoveredscotland.co.uk/usbiography/p/pontius pilate.html

23. Isaiah's Prophecies of the Messiah. (n.d.). Retrieved July 03, 2016, from http://www.agapebiblestudy.com/charts/Isaiah%27s%20Messianic%20Prophecies.htm

24. Legacy, H. (n.d.). Medicinal Qualities of Onion. Retrieved February 03, 2017, from http://www.herballegacy.com/Wilson_Medicinal.html

25. Lewis, N., & Reinhold, M. J. (1951). *Roman civilization: sourcebook II: the empire*. New York: Columbia University Press.

26. Life, Hope & Truth. (n.d.). Retrieved February 03, 2016, from https://lifehopeandtruth.com

27. Liguria - Encyclopedia. (n.d.). Retrieved April, 2016, from theodora.com/encyclopedia/l2/liguria.html

28. Maier, P. L. (1968). *Pontius Pilate*. Garden City, NY: Doubleday.

29. Mills, J. R. (2000). *Memoirs of Pontius Pilate: a novel*. Grand Rapids, MI: Fleming H. Revell.

30. Network Home. (n.d.). Retrieved July 03, 2016, from http://www.biblicalarchaeology.org

31. Orthodox England. (n.d.). Retrieved February 03, 2014, from http://www.orthodoxengland.org.uk/hp.php

32. Pontius Pilate. (n.d.). Retrieved July 03, 2016, from http://www.livius.org/articles/person/pontius-pilate

33. Pontius Pilate. (2014, November 11). Retrieved June 03, 2015, from biography.com/people/pontius-pilate-9440686

34. Roman Wines. (n.d.). Retrieved August 03, 2016, from monsaventinus.wikia.com/wiki/Roman_Wines

35. S. (2012, October 15). Quattrocchi San Michele Sicilian Shepherd Staff. Retrieved July, 2014, from http://www.youtube.com/watch?v=XBQe3_QpXV8

36. *Sion in German, French and Italian* in the online Historical Dictionary of Switzerland. http://www.hls-dhs-dss.ch/

37. Smith, William, ed. (1857). "Sedu'ni". *Dictionary of Greek and Roman Geography*. **2**. London: John Murray. p. 947.

38. The Samnites. (n.d.). Retrieved May 03, 2014, from http://www.morronedelsannio.com/eng_web/eng_sanniti.htm

39. Vermes, Geza. The authentic gospel of Jesus. London, Penguin Books. 2004.

40. Was Jesus Divine? (n.d.). Retrieved September 03, 2016, from patheos.com/blogs/markdroberts/series/was-Jesus-Divine

41. What Does Paul Say About the Resurrection of Jesus? (n.d.). Retrieved July 03, 2016, from http://www.allaboutjesuschrist.org/what-does-paul-say-about-the-resurrection-of-jesus-faq.htm

42. *What life was like when Rome ruled the world: the Roman Empire, 100 BC - AD 200*. (1997). Alexandria, VA: Time-Life Books.

43. Where Life Stories Live On. (2016, February 03). Retrieved July 03, 2016, from http://www.legacy.com

Printed in France by Amazon
Brétigny-sur-Orge, FR

18626525R00127